ISABEL COLEGATE was born in London, England. Married and the mother of three children, she now lives in Wiltshire. She is the author of four other novels, including THE SHOOTING PARTY, published in an Avon Bard edition.

Other Avon Bard Books by
Isabel Colegate

THE SHOOTING PARTY

STATUES IN A GARDEN

ISABEL COLEGATE

 A BARD BOOK/PUBLISHED BY AVON BOOKS

Front cover illustration detail from John Sargeant's
In the Luxembourg Gardens. John G. Johnson Collection,
Philadelphia, Pennsylvania.

AVON BOOKS
A division of
The Hearst Corporation
959 Eighth Avenue
New York, New York 10019

Copyright © 1964 by Isabel Colegate
Published by arrangement with the author
Library of Congress Catalog Card Number: 82-90357
ISBN: 0-380-60368-3

First Bard Printing, September, 1982

BARD TRADEMARK REG. U. S. PAT. OFF. AND IN
OTHER COUNTRIES, MARCA REGISTRADA, HECHO EN
U. S. A.

Printed in the U. S. A.

OP   10 9 8 7 6 5 4 3 2

Chapter One

The sun shone all summer. Everybody knows that.

A few hundred yards to the east of the house was a deep narrow valley, running from north to south, with wooded slopes and a thin stream at the bottom. On one of the slopes the undergrowth concealed wild strawberries: they ripened to a rare sweetness, being protected from the birds. In the night the vixen, who had two cubs in the coppice on the other side of the field, would pause in her hunting on the overgrown path between the strawberries and take the ripe ones into her delicate mouth, one by one. They had seen her from the house sometimes, slipping across the field at dusk.

Lady Londonderry saw Cynthia Weston, driving in the park.

'Of course I am not really speaking to you,' she said. 'Because of Home Rule. But I don't think anyone is looking.' (They were.) 'How is your pretty Kitty?'

'My pretty Kitty,' said Cynthia. 'Full of funny ideas, not at all like Violet. But I've got a nice girl coming as a sort of companion governess. She's become too much of a handful for poor old Miss Grainger. I suppose the year before coming out is always an awkward one. But here is Philip. How unexpected.'

Philip, her nephew and adopted son, rode up on a new horse he was exercising in the Row; and Lady Londonderry, waving a greeting to him and a farewell to Cynthia, was driven off between the ranks of green park chairs and the people in hats, who were talking and gazing.

* * *

London 1914. People said there was too much money about, the old standards were going (Rand magnates, American heiresses). Bitterness in politics, talk of civil war in Ireland, of a general strike in the autumn; suffragettes (arson, forcible feeding, broken glass, the Cat and Mouse Act); high feelings about the disestablishment of the Welsh Church, about Lloyd George's new social legislation, about the Post-Impressionists, the Russian Ballet, Ibsen, about Mrs. Patrick Campbell saying 'bloody' in *Pygmalion*. A world of possibilities, and social injustice of course, and a great deal of stolid overfed stupidity; and one could argue about what was an end and what was a beginning, but we are not concerned with that at the moment. We are not trying to recapture an age as it was, or to write history: we are trying to remember the background for a fable. A private background for a private fable.

Violet, Cynthia Weston's elder daughter, was engaged to Wilfred Moreton, the eldest son of a viscount with property in Radnorshire; but it was not yet announced, and so it came about that she sat in a supper-room and declined a young man's invitation to dine with him unchaperoned the following night and the young man said it was the fault of these dashed conventions and cried out quite passionately, 'You know what it means? It means that you are throwing us into the arms of actresses!' And Violet, sharing it in anticipation with Kitty, put back her head and laughed too loudly for decorum, and the young man, seeing the laughter in her long neck, became even more restless and quite soon left the party altogether.

Anyway, it was during the summer of 1914 that all this happened; but it might have happened at any time; at least, I suppose it might. I suppose in fact these same events take place all the time in one shape or another, or might take place, and it is only the human inclination for myth which requires them to have happened once and for all, at some specific moment in time; but then I am not sure that I can always tell the difference between an idea and an event, which may lead to confusion, so we had better confine ourselves to events. Because the particulars, the people, the scandal, all that really did happen, and in dealing with that, we shall, I suppose, know where we are.

(I know it happened because I was there; but in quite a subsidiary capacity, and it was a long time ago.)

Cynthia had forgotten to tell her husband what time Alice Benedict was arriving, and the servants, who did know, had not reminded him because they thought he also knew; so that Aylmer and his mother were still in the dining-room when somone came in and said, 'Miss Benedict is here.'

'Miss who?' They were in the middle of an argument and did not want to be interrupted.

'Miss Benedict, Sir Aylmer. The young lady who is to look after Miss Kitty.'

'Of course, how stupid of me.' He rose hurriedly to his feet. 'We'll have our coffee in the library—oh we've had coffee?—we'll have some more then. I'm sure Miss Benedict would like some.' He was already out in the hall and shaking her hand. 'I am so sorry to keep you waiting. I had rather forgotten the time of your train, just for the moment. We were involved in an argument. My mother's political views are so extreme that I tend to forget the passage of time in trying to refute them. But you haven't met my mother. Miss Benedict—Mrs. Weston.'

The old woman shook her hand, looked at her rather piercingly and said, 'I'm sorry you have been kept waiting.'

'But I've only been here a few moments. And I have been looking round me. It's so pretty.'

'It is pleasant in the evening. Have they shown you your room? Then come in and have some coffee.' Mrs. Weston led the way into the library, which the evening sun had just left.

Later, Alice Benedict wrote to her mother and father. Her father was a dean in Dublin.

'I am delighted with the whole idea,' she wrote, 'and bursting with impolite curiosity and, I'm afraid, the usual thing, unbounded admiration. They really do seem, in spite of being so grand, to be so good as well—and clever. The whole house speaks of it. I haven't seen Kitty yet because she was already in bed, but they talked about her and she sounds fun. Old Mrs. Weston seems to be very fond of her, and amused by her; he rather more worried. Apparently she is an ardent Suffragist! Mrs. Weston is rather alarming, very much a wonderful old lady. She certainly looks it and dresses it, but her conversation is perhaps too acid exactly to fit the role. She uses foreign phrases quite a lot, like Aunt Mildred, but with a better French accent—and German as well. When I came they had been arguing about politics and afterwards he teased her about some German called Marks that she had been quoting—but fancy keeping his political faith alive like that and arguing about it—isn't that good when he has been in the thing so long? The house is beautiful—and roses climbing all over the trees outside just beginning to come out—I thought I was driving into a fairy story when I arrived—perhaps I was. Lady Weston is in London but returns tomorrow. She must look even more beautiful here than she did when I saw her in London. There is a picture of her in the hall by Boldini—very dramatic but too fashionable-looking—he has missed the spirituality of her face.'

Old Mrs. Weston, who slept little, was walking in the upper part of the garden, wrapped in a shawl. The vixen was crossing the field, returning to her cubs.

Chapter Two

Aylmer Weston was a Liberal politician, and a member of Asquith's Cabinet.

He had first entered the House of Commons in 1894, three years after coming down from Oxford where he had been a Balliol scholar. He had also been President of the Union, won the Craven and Ireland scholarships and ended with First Class Honours in Classical Moderations and Greats; so that a certain amount was expected of him even in that age of scholar statesmen. He was made a Fellow of All Souls in 1903, while he was still building up a successful practice at the Bar; in 1906, when the Liberals came into power, he abandoned his career as a barrister and accepted office; in 1908 Asquith made him a member of his Cabinet.

His father had been a grand old man of Liberalism, and Aylmer's career had, at first at any rate, suffered from his being unfavourably compared with his father, on grounds not of intelligence nor of honesty but of 'character'. As well as his political traditions, he had inherited from his father his small estate in Wiltshire and his way of life as a member of the minor gentry. The house there was beautifully placed and showed the marks of years of care and discriminating affection, so that impressionable visitors like Alice Benedict gasped and became enthusiastic. Aylmer and Cynthia had three children, Edmund, Violet and Kitty, and a nephew, Philip, whom they had adopted in his childhood on the death of his parents in India. They entertained a good deal, not only because Aylmer's position required it, but because Cynthia had become a famous hostess.

Cynthia arrived the day after Alice Benedict. She had stayed in London to dine with the Asquiths for the Monds' dance in Lowndes Square: Aylmer, who had recently had a bad attack of bronchitis, had been told by his doctor to take things quietly and had come home to the country instead of going with her. He was feeling a little guilty about this, and making a special effort to show interest in her evening.

'I was amused,' she reassured him. 'But you were quite right not to come. It was hot and crowded.'

'Was Maud there, and Reggie? You took Violet?'

'She came with the Moretons, looking very sweet. Everyone seems to know about the engagement, so it's just as well it's to be in the paper on Tuesday. Of course congratulations everywhere, and everyone seems to agree that he's a nice boy and a good match. Poor Daisy Bellew couldn't conceal her dismay—those two huge daughters still on her hands.'

'She couldn't have had hopes of Wilfred?'

'One has hopes of everybody when one is as frantic as that.'

'Are they joining us today, the young people?'

'Wilfred is driving her down after lunch, with Trotter. Poor Trotter, she hates the back of that car. And the Tamworths are coming this afternoon, too. That's all—we shall be quiet. Tell me, what do you think of our Miss Benedict? Is she going to be all right?'

'I'm delighted with what I have seen of her. She seems a most intelligent and reasonable young woman. And Kitty and she seem to get on well. When I was in the garden this morning they came dashing past me at top speed, showing their knees and laughing like children, going to see the owl's nest. It was charming.'

'She's supposed to stop Kitty showing her knees, not show hers too. Metaphorically speaking, I mean.'

'But first she has to let her know she's on her side. She told me as much herself. I think she'll be a success.'

'You don't think she's too pretty, do you? I mean—Philip?'

Aylmer shook his head. 'She's got too much sense.'

'That's what I thought too. Philip is coming tonight by the way.'

'Is he? That's unusual. Have his Bohemian friends not asked him away?'

'It seems not. And Edmund will be here too of course.'

He looked at her, and smiled. 'I have heard that mothers prefer their bad sons to their good.'

'Philip is not my son,' she said quickly, then, in explanation, 'I feel the difference so much. Lately in fact I have been feeling I don't even know him very well.'

He nodded. 'I feel the same. He is something new to me. Edmund is totally familiar.'

'I know. Philip puzzles me very much. You don't think he has changed lately?'

'I think he is having a turbulent youth, that's all. He's always been difficult.'

'You don't think he has changed towards us?'

'I don't know. I suppose they do change. One can only remain the same towards them oneself and hope for the best. His situation here is not intrinsically easy. He's always been a bit jealous of Edmund. Perhaps now that he is making friends and a life of his own he will calm down, relax the tension.'

'Perhaps if he and Edmund had not both gone to Eton . . . ?' she said. 'Edmund was more liked.'

'He would have taken it as a slight if we had sent him somewhere else. Perhaps his new friends will make him use his mind more than they ever managed to at school. A little intellectual discipline would do him a world of good. But let's not bother him about it. He has been away so long that we must be careful to welcome him without reproach. Besides, it will be nice to see him.'

'Of course. I love him, as you know. But some people are easier to love than others. Never mind. I'm afraid I bought some silly fans yesterday. I didn't really need them but I was getting tired of my old ones, and they are rather pretty. Would you like to see them?'

'Very much. And then could we walk round the garden before lunch? Gibbon wants to know what you are going to decide about the new rose beds, and after lunch I must get to work on this speech.'

Philip stood outside the window. He looked in without being seen. They have not seen me, he thought. They are in some drawing-room comedy, in artificial sunlight, talking irrelevantly. They are a group, but an irrelevant group. I am relevant. I know what they do not know. I know myself; therefore I know them, and know them to be liars.

Why is she never alone? Why does she only subsist in a web of chatter, spinning it all around her as she sews at her absurd embroidery? She makes a web to hide behind and when the sun shines on it looks as if it were made of brilliance, but when the sun goes there is nothing there at all. I am going to be irritated, I am going to behave badly. What an insult it is, their phantasmagorical self-confidence. Is it that which is making me hesitate behind the vines? All I want is to set her free.

The Tamworths—rhymes after dinner—oh God, not that, not rhymes after dinner? A new face, smiling, but silent—of course, the new governess—interesting?—not modest enough for a governess—mouth too big—possibilities—yes—spin your web, my great white love, I shall be upstairs tumbling the governess.

He laughed and stepped into the room.

Cynthia was sewing, listening to Kitty talking too much as usual, aware that Aylmer opposite her was wondering whether it was too soon to go back to the library and get on with his speech. The governess removed Kitty's empty tea-cup, thereby gently interrupting the flow of her talk.

Cynthia was pleased. Kitty and the governess usually had tea with them when they were alone and since the Tamworths were old friends she had not banished them in their honour. She approved of Miss Benedict's bearing, unobtrusive, yet not, as poor Miss Grainger's used to be, aggressively so.

And then the short familiar laugh and Philip stepped in through the garden door and Cynthia stood up eagerly to embrace him and say, 'How lovely. I was afraid something must have happened. Kitty, ring for some more tea. How well you look. It's lovely to see you.'

He greeted Aylmer and old Mrs. Weston, shook hands with the Tamworths, Violet, Wilfred, was introduced to Miss Benedict, patted Edmund on the back and kissed Kitty, who said, 'Why were you laughing?'

'A concept,' he said. He put his hands on her shoulders and held her away from him. 'Well, well. Little Kitty. Prettier every day I swear.'

She kicked him sharply on the shin. 'I knew you'd say that,' she said, pleased.

He rubbed his ankle. 'Oh Miss Benedict, you haven't improved her at all. You'll have to be stricter.'

'Kitty, Kitty,' her father mildly remonstrated, and stood up. 'I've got a speech to get out of the way. Come and smoke a cigarette with me when you've had some tea, Philip. I'll be in the library.'

'I will.' Philip opened the door for him. 'How's the Bar, Edmund? And the wedding plans, Violet? I want to hear all your news.'

He sat down. Miss Benedict with a polite glance at Cynthia quietly left the room. Cynthia, smiling, began to pour out his tea.

Alice went upstairs to the schoolroom and sat down at the desk.

'So now I have met them all,' she wrote quickly (she knew that Kitty would soon be coming up, when the dressing bell went). 'There are also staying here some people called Tamworth. He is tall, handsome, bearded, polite, and I thought rather amusing, but Kitty says he is an old bore and thinks of nothing but rhyming games (he has some quite high position in the Treasury so this can't be the whole truth). Lady Tamworth is like a little monkey, always chattering and scratching. She is dressed in strange bright colours, rather oriental-looking, and seems to know all about everything. "But, my dears, didn't you know, what really happened was . . ."—I think half of her stories are made up and this may be the point of them, but I can't understand all of what she says and find her extremely terrifying. There is another person coming in time for dinner. Her name is Margaret something and she is Violet's greatest friend. Kitty says she is feeble (but then so are we all, who don't belong to the WSPU). Violet is pretty and small, not much like her mother. She is beautifully dressed and has lovely fair hair and a tiny mouth like a button. She seems very happy about her engagement and to think of little else. There is some talk of her fiancé's regiment having to go to India, so they may put the wedding forward. He is big, has a loud laugh, talks mostly of horses, or shooting.

'Now, where have I got to? Oh yes, Edmund. Edmund is exactly like his father, though smaller and thinner—but the same long nose and melancholy good looks, made less melancholy by the same sweet smile. The both make me feel—what?—that if I told them my true thoughts they would be shocked, though kind—and yet they both must know far worse things than my true thoughts, mustn't they? He is reading for the Bar.

'Then there is Philip—dark and white-faced—their nephew who has lived here since he was a boy. Kitty loves him because he encourages her iconoclasm. He looks bitter, interesting, and the opposite of Edmund. I think he has what you might call a roving eye. He is in the Army, but Kitty says he does not like it. On Monday or Tuesday they will all go away again and there will only be Kitty and me and old Mrs. Weston. Then we can try to do some reading! Old Mrs. Weston is fun to talk to, though her grim oracular pronouncements are sometimes a little unnerving. But according to Kitty she approves of me, so I hope we shall . . .'

Here Kitty came in, holding a bunch of yellow roses. 'Gloire de Dijon. Do you like roses?'

'Of course. But I know hardly any of their names.'

'Nor do I. But this one is called Gloire de Dijon. Why are you always writing? It can't be a letter home every time. I know. You are not really Alice Benedict. You are Charlotte

Brontë. And you are going to write a frightfully fascinating novel in which you and Father elope together. Isn't that it?'

Philip went into Cynthia's bedroom as her maid was pinning up her hair.

'You don't mind my coming in? You're always surrounded at every other moment of the day.'

'Surrounded? Nonsense. Not down here. Here we are always quiet. But sit down, do. This is a long business, isn't it, Beatrice? What do you think of Wilfred? You'd hardly met him, had you?'

'Once or twice in London. He seems nice enough. Just the thing for Violet. Are they really going to be married in July? It will be a terrible rush for you, won't it?'

'It will rather, but if his regiment is really likely to be sent to India I think we shall have to do it for them. Naturally they want to get married before he goes. But it's yourself you've come to talk about. How are you? Are you happy?'

'Do I always talk about myself then? I suppose I do. Yes, I'm happy.'

'But what?'

'But I'm wondering whether I'm cut out for the Army. Somehow I seem to be moving in a different sort of direction. None of my friends are in the regiment now; they're all outside, in other fields. I feel I ought to be doing something less stereotyped, if you see what I mean. One ought to do what one likes, oughtn't one, in other words what one can fulfil oneself in doing. Don't you agree?'

'Of course. If you mean by that finding out how best you can serve your country and your fellow men.'

'Oh Cynthia, Cynthia.' He looked in the mirror at her serious beautiful face. 'Not making my fortune, and enjoying it if I can?'

'I'm sure we mean the same thing,' she said, though she looked puzzled. 'But what do you think—what would you like to do instead?'

'Don't look so serious. There's no hurry about any of this. But I've got a friend who is in business, in the City . . .'

'Oh a bank, you mean, something like that?'

'Well—that sort of thing. But it's all in the air, you un-

14

derstand. I mean, as regards my part in it, if any. I'm just turning it over in my mind.'

'I don't know,' she said. 'You mean you would resign your commission. Well, if you really think it would be a wise thing to do . . . Have you talked to Aylmer about it?'

'No. I thought I would wait until I had something rather more definite to suggest.'

'As long as you don't do anything rash, without consulting him. But tell me more about this friend.'

'I'd like to but I think it will have to wait, because there's the first bell. Perhaps tomorrow? But will you not mention it to Aylmer just yet? Would you mind?'

'No, I don't mind. Thank you, Beatrice. But don't forget that his advice can be valuable.' The maid left the room, but Cynthia stayed sitting in front of the mirror for a moment. 'He is very experienced, you know. I think he would be able to help you.'

'I know.' He seemed to have lost interest in the subject, to be looking round the room at her things, her furniture, her Chinese silk wrap at the end of her bed, in search of something else to talk about.

She still gazed at her reflection in the mirror, serious.

He looked at it too. 'Oh Cynthia, you are very beautiful. I wish I were your son.'

Her eyes opened wide.

'But you are.'

He shook his head. 'No. I should feel safer if I were.'

'Safer?' She bent her head, fastening a bracelet on her wrist. 'You are safe.' She turned to look at him, the mirror behind her. 'Don't be so self-doubting. Of course you are safe. We are all safe—as safe as anyone can be who has got to die some day—and we can surely hope, if we have not lost touch with God, to be safe even then. Philip, you haven't done anything wrong, have you?'

'Anything wrong?' He looked surprised, then amused. 'Nothing against the law.'

'Because you know we are here to help you. You wouldn't conceal anything like that from us, would you?'

He shook his head hopelessly. 'No, no.'

She persevered. 'I thought it might be that something was making you feel guilty. Because if you have nothing to be ashamed of, you see, it seems to me that nothing

15

should be holding you back from—well, from doing anything you like. From taking, in all confidence, what is offered by life. We have such luck. We are born in a lucky age for people of our class. We have such opportunities to be happy and to do good. If we remember our responsibilities and can keep our self-respect, what is there to spoil life?' She wanted to communicate her own confidence.

'Is this what Aylmer tells you?'

'Of course. It is what he believes.'

'But, Cynthia, you don't know what it's all about, you don't know what life is like. No, I mean . . . you are what Aylmer has made you. You're different really, you don't know how different you are.'

She was very reasonable. 'Even if I am as Aylmer made me, I nevertheless *am* what Aylmer has made me. Everybody is made into something one way or another, and women of course by their husbands. Why not?' She smiled at him.

'But . . .' He turned away. 'Oh well . . .' He turned back, smiled, took her hand and looked at it. 'Who will make me then?'

She said seriously, 'I expect you will have to make yourself.'

'Why are your hands so white?'

'Beatrice makes some stuff with lemon juice in it which she puts on them. Philip, are you . . . ? I wish I knew what really was bothering you.'

'I am not bothered, I am not bothered. I want to hurt your hand.'

She laid her other hand gently on the back of his. 'No, no. I believe that's all you want, to hurt me. That's why you're saying this, whatever it is you are saying. Oh Philip, you are very trying. Now we're late. Come along.' She put her hand on his arm.

'I'm sorry. I'll behave very well for the rest of the evening.'

Harbingers of violence in the violet dusk, Miss Ada Thompson and Miss Clara Pease-Henneky lurked in the bushes by the drive. Gazing at the softly golden house, they relished the thought of the fright they would give it. They did not know that they were not alone, that the rabbit was wandering down the hillside behind them to be

16

slaughtered by the fox, that the blackbird's unwinking eye was not a foot from their felt hats as she sat on her five warm eggs, that the blunt-headed owl was above them on moth-soft wings, night-hunting too. But perhaps they felt it, because they trembled and breathed faster, in their hats and skirts become elemental.

Chapter Three

Lord Tamworth, taking Cynthia in to dinner, said. 'How charming it always looks in here. And how often I have argued back and forth across this table.'

'You're so sweet the way you don't mind being plunged into a noisy family party. But tonight we are going to be very quiet and restrained.'

'Are we? Oh dear.'

'Yes, because it's such a lovely evening. I think we could have a little of that window open, Bartlett. I don't think it will blow out the candles. To think it is only May.'

'I fear it can't last, as early as this, and we shall have rain. Is your tennis court in use yet?'

'Yes. We must play tomorrow.'

'Aylmer's too good for me. I think I shall stick to croquet.'

'He's out of practice. He's played hardly at all this year. Really he does more bicycling than tennis for exercise.'

'Ah, *la bicyclette*. I must tell you an amusing story about a "biking" episode. It happened when we were staying with . . .'

Lady Tamworth at the other end of the table: 'Of course it is said of him that he is a careerist, but I can never understand why that should be supposed to be shocking in a politician. What else could he be?'

Aylmer: 'Ah now, that is a bait to which I shall have to rise. He could be many other things. Let's agree first on what we mean by a careerist . . .'

Margaret James to Philip: 'Have you been to the Academy yet?'

'No. Have you?'

'I went to the Private View on Friday. I thought it was not so good this year as last.'

'Impossible!'

'Didn't you think last year's was good then?'

'I didn't see it.'

'You don't much care for Art?'

'I care very much.'

'Ah then, I know, you are advanced. You like Kokoschka and that sort of thing, don't you? There, you are amazed that I've heard of him. As a matter of fact I don't know anything about his pictures. I just keep his name at the back of my mind to confound people with. Never mind, let us compromise with the Russian Ballet. I am sure we can agree on that, can't we?'

'Of course. It's marvellous.'

'Isn't it? And isn't Nijinsky frightfully fascinating? And wasn't the décor for Scheherazade simply the most divine thing in the world?'

Violet to Edmund: 'And how are they, the friends, let loose at last on the world? Or are they still sheltered, still pretending to be at Cambridge?'

'Only when we are alone. Only then do we dare to expose our unshakeable sense of our own superiority. The rest of the time we pretend to think we are just like anyone else.'

'I heard that Francis Maude had gone to South Africa. I am afraid you will sustain other losses.'

'I hope they won't be real losses. Maude is a good correspondent. Charles is going back to Cambridge, to King's, to be a don.'

'Father will be sorry. He was the one he most hoped would go into politics.'

'He may not have become irretrievably academic. But I think he will stay there. He cares too much for the pursuit of the realities in his own subject, and for his relationships with his friends, to have time for politics. They are getting more and more demanding, you know. Manners, by the way, was quite *bouleversé* when I told him of your engagement. I suppose you had been leading him up the garden path.'

'Not in the least. I only met him once or twice. I did

think him very amusing. But he spits. I would never lead up the garden path a man who spits.'

'Really? He spits? By accident, you mean, or design?'

'Oh, accident, I suppose. I mean, when he speaks. I don't mean what you might call a therapeutical spit.'

'Look out, or you'll start spitting yourself. Hasn't Wilfred cured you of the giggling habit yet?'

'No, but he's tried. He thinks I'm flippant. Through being fashionable, he says.'

'He's quite right, too. No, no, all right, I know it isn't in the least true of you, and anyway it's fun to do a little of it, but I'm glad in a way that you and Wilfred, when you marry, won't be too much in the thick of things. It's hard to limit, that's the trouble. Someone like your admirer Manners I mean—if one spends all one's time in dancing and gambling and mad parties there's no time for anything else—and yet, once one starts getting asked of course it's fun and one doesn't refuse. Now you're going to say I'm being pompous, but really one does have to try and strike the balance—so much to do and so little time, and all that.'

'Not *so* little time, poor old thing, is there? Or do you mean, so little time before your Bar Finals?'

'Partly that. In fact I'm thinking of taking a week or two off while you're all up in London and coming down here to bury myself in my books.'

'That's just because you love it so much here, nothing to do with work. Besides you'll get no peace from Kitty.'

'The new governess will keep her occupied. I like her, don't you? Miss Benedict, I mean.'

'Awfully. I wonder why she's a governess. Is there some sad story, do you think?'

'How romantic you are. What sort of story do you think—a wicked stepmother?'

'A cad. A monstrous cad who let her down.'

A fish *soufflé*, the palest gold, intricately decorated with prawns and parsley. Lady Tamworth protested, 'It's too pretty to break into,' but broke into it none the less.

Wilfred Moreton was sitting on old Mrs. Weston's deaf side, so their conversation was slightly disjointed.

'I used to know someone who lived in Radnorshire, must be a neighbour of yours. A general, fought in the Crimea, made a frightful fool of himself, I believe.'

'I can't think of any generals in our immediate neighbourhood . . .'

'That will be him, yes. Terrible old bore, isn't he? It was his wife I used to like. Carmelita she was called. Made her own divided skirts long before they came into fashion. Can't think why she married him. I suppose she thought it would be a life of adventure.'

'Ah well, they say a soldier's life . . .'

'Aren't they? Absolute frights, as often as not. Though it's very detached of you to say so since you are just about to make our poor Violet one.'

'Make her a—? Oh yes. Yes, yes, yes, I see. A soldier's wife. Yes, rather.'

'Or don't you see her in that light?'

'I certainly do. Not that that's the reason—well, I mean—I know she will make a perfect soldier's wife but that's just my jolly luck. I should have asked her to marry me if she had been the least likely to be so of any woman in the world.'

'You wouldn't. Because you wouldn't have fallen in love with her.'

'I most certainly should.'

'No, you would not have been drawn to her had she not been cut out to be a soldier's wife. Love is much more a question of convenience than you think.'

'Not at all. I won't be shaken in my faith in love.'

'Nor will I. It's the only faith I have. But I don't look on it in quite your light. But tell me—I hear you are a great sportsman?'

Cynthia laughed at a scandal from Lord Tamworth.

'I shouldn't have told you, I thought you knew,' he said in mock embarrassment. 'I should never have told you, had I not thought you suspected.'

'Nonsense. It wouldn't have been nearly such fun for you if I had.'

'But I am not as a rule a *faiseur d'embarras*, now am I? Am I not the soul of discretion, of propriety, of decorum?'

'But of course!' And Philip asked me for something and I did not know what it was he was asking for and so I could not give it to him. But I would give him anything. 'Is he looking well, do you think, or rather pale?'

'Who is this? Oh, your nephew. He looks well enough

to me.' Why do so many voices become reserved at Philip's name? 'Bit of a gambler, isn't he?'

'Not excessively, I believe.'

'I hear good things of Edmund on many sides. I think he's going to carry on his father's work, you know—he's really sound, I believe. It's a great thing when they turn out like that.'

'I know. Oh, I know.'

Philip: Now she is suddenly clouded, her eyes down, frowning slightly. Is it something I said before dinner? Good. I wanted to cloud her. But not to make her lower her eyes. Why hasn't he noticed, why does he never notice her moods, why does he treat her like a mirror, a pretty little mirror, when she could burn him to a cinder if once she would show him her own image instead of his? Oh yes, Miss James, yes, I will play. What do you like to play? Charades? I will take you out to tea at Rumpelmeyer's. But I am quite ineligible, you know. My father had very little to leave me, and though my kind uncle provides for me, he has a son younger than I am, who will inherit everything. I wonder if you do know. Perhaps you do. Perhaps you think it is safe to flirt with me, to show me how light and frivolous you are, because I am a detrimental and do not matter. How little she knows. How little she knows how little I matter. Oh lovely violence, make some move!

Mrs. Weston, putting on her stern old lady's voice: 'Brooding, brooding? How is your reading?'

Philip: 'What's wrong with brooding? And I have read nothing, except Bernhardi. I look at pictures instead.'

'What an extraordinary choice. What can have led you to him? A cheap militarist, a common pamphleteer—what made you read him?'

'Someone recommended it to me. I can't say I cared for it greatly, though of course blood and iron makes sense in international relations.'

'Does it indeed! Bernhardi! Well! Nietzsche, if you like, though I'd rather read Hegel myself. Look here, perhaps I could recommend you one or two books which might interest you?'

* * *

Candles. Rosewood. Silver. Pale tulips. Dear Violet, I would like to tell you, Edmund thought, about how touched I am by the thought of your marriage and how ardently I wish you to be happy, and how I wish that I too might find a companion with whom to begin a long to and fro of love. Wilfred's an ass of course. Still, an honourable and loving ass. And dear Violet for all her charm is no brilliant intellect. I expect they will do very well. Oh God, let them do very well. 'Oh no, you flatter me, Lady Tamworth. I spend my whole time at my studies.'

'Edmund, what a barefaced lie. I hear of nothing but your conquests. Lady Curzon told me that pretty little Anna Forbes who was in her party the other night. . .'

Now I have a moment's peace, at the head of my table, thought Aylmer. Enid Tamworth is busy with Edmund, Margaret with Philip—they have talked a good deal this evening—perhaps if Philip were to marry and settle down? But he is hardly in a position to, and anyway she strikes me as rather a foolish little creature. He could do better. I think I am improving in one respect, that is that I am better able to pause and savour things instead of involving myself in them so blindly that it is only afterwards that I realize what in fact they were. Cynthia said the other day she thought I was becoming too detached—over Ireland that was—but I detach myself in order to see. Amusing, old Tammy, he puts on such a performance all the time—yet it is all very agreeable—a lightweight, though, for all his good brain. She'd have made a good wife for a more outstanding man. They suit each other well enough, though. Two letters, but I think I can do these tomorrow. Bed early perhaps. Thucydides. I think I made my position clear to Asquith on Thursday. It's no use being blackmailed by Carson and his crew. But I shall not think about that tonight. Edmund. Has he enough stamina? Have I? Oh yes, I am very steady these days. Pretty Violet. Cynthia will cry a great deal about the first wedding in the family. Wilfred's an ass of course. But quite a sound ass. I am not feeling sentimental this evening after all. I thought for a moment I was. But no. Merely content. I shall plead overwork, escape early, go to bed, read Thucydides.

Violet and Lord Tamworth were talking about Venice,

Aylmer lightly extolling to Miss James the virtues of Balzac. Plump *poussins* dressed up in watercress, silver lids removed to expose the mounds of baked mashed potato; Mrs. Weston on Schopenhauer, Philip not listening; Wilfred, now more animated, telling Cynthia about the wing span of the albatross; Lady Tamworth giving a sparkling account of the late King's death-bed . . . 'and the minute she let her in—the Queen, I mean, let Mrs. Keppel in—the *minute*, my dear, before she'd even shut the bedroom door . . .' A crash. A splintering. A silence.

'Sit down, Philip,' said Aylmer quietly. 'What is it, Bartlet?'

The butler, moving aside the curtain, picked up the brick and brought it to Aylmer, holding it in front of him so that he could read the note which was fastened to it by an elastic band and which said, VOTES FOR WOMEN!

A footman came in and spoke quietly to the butler, who passed on the message to Aylmer.

'No, no, let them go,' said Aylmer. 'Tell James to escort them politely—*politely*—to the gate. He had better take Mrs. Parsons with him as chaperon.' Turning to Lady Tamworth, he said, 'I'm so sorry. I fear that must be an effect of my speech last week. You didn't know you were coming to such a dangerous house.'

Edmund said, 'Father, I wonder whether someone ought just to have a look round outside—you know, in case?'

'Yes. Barlett, ask them to inspect the stables and outbuildings and see they're all right, would you?'

Margaret James flushed suddenly. 'Arson! How can they be so wicked?'

'Oh I don't suppose we shall find anything so dramatic here. I don't think they are wicked—but very, very mistaken. They merely do harm to their own cause. They've caught a taste for violence, that's all.'

The next course was presented, a *crème brulée* (Mrs. Browne did them beautifully). It muffled immediately the little incident; which had, after all, amounted to nothing.

Chapter Four

Miss Ada Thompson and Miss Clara Pease-Henneky slept in the train. Being ignored was not stimulating. They rattled through the night towards Paddington, towards—for they achieved it in the end—Holloway and hunger-strike, towards, respectively, the Ambulance Corps and a munitions factory, for changing the direction though not the blindness of their loyalties, they did awfully well in the war.

We all did, I suppose, except Philip.

At Charleswood everyone slept too, more comfortably. Except for old Mrs. Weston, who wandered about the garden as usual, hearing the nightingales in the valley and the shriek of the rabbit as the vixen killed it for her cubs, and thinking of death and despising herself for the littleness of her understanding.

Chapter Five

By Tuesday morning they had all gone, except for Kitty, Alice and old Mrs. Weston.

Before he left Philip said to Aylmer, 'There's something I'd rather like to discuss with you. I somehow haven't had a chance, and anyway it's a little difficult. I wonder if I might see you this week some time, if you could spare me a moment?'

'Of course. Let me see, why not dine with me on Thursday at the House? We've got questions on the Budget resolutions coming up and I shall have to be there all evening. Cynthia is taking Violet to something or other, I forget what. Come along about eight, would you?'

So he came along about eight, came along the corridor past the deferential policeman and the immensity of Westminster Hall, and waited in the central lobby while an official took his card in to Aylmer, and saw Harry Chaplin, a great blond amazing figure who breezily shouted that he was going to give Lloyd George hell over the Budget, and

Masterman, Aylmer's friend, looking untidy and ill, and Arthur Balfour who most politely sent his regards to Cynthia, 'whom I believe, I truly believe, to be the most beautiful woman in London'; and then a red-haired young woman, rather pretty but flustered, asked him if he knew where she might find Mr. Churchill and he directed her with great authority though total ignorance, and thought afterwards perhaps she was going to throw a bomb. Then at last he saw Aylmer, a figure here of benign authority, despite his comparative youth, stooping slightly, smiling a mild short-sighted smile, having not yet seen him, beautifully dressed in his dark coat and pin-striped trousers, which never seemed to crumple through the longest, roughest, session, his hair very sleek and statesmanlike, a little grey. He caught sight of Philip and hurried towards him.

'I hope you haven't been waiting. Come along in. We might as well dine straight away, don't you think? We've got quite a quiet day today, thank heavens, after yesterday, but I have to hang around because there's an education thing coming up later which may affect me. The Local Government boys are at it at the moment. Strange that one should regard a Lloyd George budget as a respite from anything, isn't it? But there have been such scenes over this wretched Irish business, one gets quite worn out with it.'

'What's going to happen about that?' asked Philip, walking quickly to keep pace with Aylmer.

'We'll put the Home Rule Bill on the statute book and follow immediately with an amending Bill, but it's a question of what Redmond can get his rank and file to agree to. Here we are. Now where's our table? Ah good. Have a glass of sherry first of all and let's take our time.'

Accepting, Philip thought how brisk he was here, and perhaps a little self-important; but then he was ready to take that back as Aylmer gave an immense yawn and tipped back his chair. The truth is, thought Philip, I can't even get him there: he is brisk because he has just come from his work, but he will calm down, he will give me—don't I know it?—his sincere and undivided attention. In due course, when I raise the matter. For he, naturally, will not refer to the fact that I have asked myself here in order to discuss something with him.

'We thought we might see you last night,' Aylmer was saying.

'I wasn't asked,' said Philip.

'Good heavens, I thought you were so much in demand these days.'

'No, that's Edmund. How was it?'

'I was only there a very short time, to be honest. We dined *chez* Cunard, which was amusing. Have you seen Edmund? No? I wondered what luck he had had at that sale he was going to. There was a good sale of porcelain at Christie's, I gather. I rather think he was hoping to pick up something pretty for Violet.'

'Cynthia will be very busy over the wedding.'

Philip's parents had died of cholera when he was eight. His father, Aylmer's brother, had been in the Indian Civil Service. Philip had gone to live with his youthful aunt and uncle and it had somehow come about that he had called them neither aunt and uncle nor mother and father but simply by their Christian names, perhaps because he had heard of them thus from his parents, having himself only seen them once, when he was a baby. In the early days, when they had been only anxious to avoid his being unhappy, they had not imposed the prefix: anyway it had been their intention that he should learn to call them mother and father, but this he had never done. At that time, when even great friends among men often addressed each other by their surnames only, it was odder than it would be now for such familiarity to exist between a young man in his late twenties and two people in their forties. No one who knew them well noticed it any more, but with others Aylmer occasionally felt a twinge of embarrassment on Cynthia's behalf. Philip liked the habit, he always had, it gave him a feeling of superiority over Edmund.

'She will enjoy it' said Aylmer. 'We must only try and stop her from enjoying it so much that she tires herself out.'

'Yes,' said Philip. 'I wanted to talk to you about myself, I am afraid. I hope it won't—well—displease you. The thing is, to put it bluntly, I'm rather fed up with the Army.'

'Oh are you?'

'You look pleased.'

'Not exactly. Go on.'

'I didn't expect you to be pleased. I thought you would be shocked.'

'You haven't told me yet what you want to do about it. I may be shocked by that. But why should I be shocked by your not liking the Army? I am a Liberal after all, and it is hardly the most liberal of professions. We thought it might make an interesting and adventurous life for you, one for which you might be fitted, but as far as I remember it was you yourself who were most in favour of the scheme.'

'It was, I know. I thought it was what I needed. I was attracted by the idea of action. But I see so little of it. I spend my time in social fripperies, accompanied by noisy aristocrats who think of nothing but gambling and actresses.'

'Ah, your Nonconformist blood coming out. Splendid, splendid! This is really delightful. I can't tell you how pleased I am about it.' He was indeed sitting up, alert with pleasure. 'You thought I should be shocked? This is good news, good. Unexpected. What do you want to do instead? Certainly you should send in your papers, even if everybody does think at first that there's been some scandal. There hasn't been by the way, has there?'

'Of course not.'

'Of course not. I shouldn't have asked. But we haven't seen as much of you as we'd have liked this last year or two, and sometimes we think you're rather a mystery to us. Well, well, and what are you thinking of? Writing?'

'Well . . .'

'I know those are rather the sort of people you've been seeing. Look here, I know Spender well and he's a first-class journalist. He could tell you all the ropes. Or isn't that it? I know it isn't politics, though I wish it were. What about the Colonial Service? Or are you going to go the whole way and go into the Church? Oh, this is splendid!'

'No, no, do stop, you're getting carried away. I don't want to do any of those things. I want to go into business and make a lot of money.'

'Oh.'

'But why not?'

'But why?' He looked absurdly put out. 'It's not that there's anything wrong with it. It's just that—well—what do you want the money for?'

'Want it for? Why, to spend!'

27

'On gambling and actresses?'

A pause.

'Possibly,' said Philip.

'Have you a business in mind?'

'Yes. I know a man called Horgan, a South African who made a lot of money there and who has now started a stockbroking firm in London. He's willing to let me go in with him.'

'I should very much like to meet him. Is he the sort of person you could bring down to stay?'

'I think a meeting in London might be better.'

'Is there a Mrs. Horgan?'

'No.'

'Ask him to dine or lunch with me, won't you? And I'll make a few inquiries in the meantime. I have some friends in the City, though not many of one's friends are stockbrokers. However, there is no reason why that should deter you. You really think that you would find this an interesting and rewarding life?'

'I hope it would be rewarding. Financially, anyway.'

'Yes. But then you have a little money of your own, and, as you know, we intend to leave you something, though of course the bulk has to go to Edmund, because of Charleswood and all that. All the same you are not likely to become destitute. Have you been losing money gambling?'

'No. I'm not unlucky, on the whole.'

'Then I don't think you have any need to do this just for the money.'

'Money matters very much though, doesn't it?' said Philip. 'What would you have done if you hadn't had it?'

'I didn't have very much. I had to earn it, at the Bar, like many others.'

'The law doesn't attract me. And anyway Edmund is doing that. But you will admit then the need to make it, the necessity? One is nothing without it.'

'You would have been something with a military career and a small independent income. I agree that money has become too important a consideration in society within the last few years, and I regret that, and I should like to see more even distribution of the new wealth, but it is by no means the only consideration. We should be in a sad way if it were.'

There was a pause, then Aylmer went on, 'Of course we shall support you in anything you really want to do, as long as you don't rush into it without finding out all about it first.'

'That's very good of you.'

Aylmer persevered. 'We do want you to find your place, you know, your object, whatever it may be. Cynthia and I both want to help you in any way we can, and if this backing of your judgment is what you need, then we shall want to do it for our own satisfaction. Edmund has always been so much more certain of what he wants than you, and though things are perhaps easier because more obvious for him, there is more scope in a way for you. You are extraordinarily free. You have a little money, a decent education, a certain background, the assurance of whatever we can offer in the way of interest and support . . .'

'I know, I know.' Philip moved a little impatiently, smiled awkwardly. 'Perhaps it would be better if I had less. I have too much perhaps, and am still in a way . . .' He stopped. He had nearly said 'excluded', which would have embarrassed them both. He went on, 'It's as you say. Things are more obvious for Edmund.'

'They will become more obvious for you. They always do. And when you have made this famous fortune you can buy up a much grander estate than anything Edmund will come into. And then you must come into Parliament and outshine him there too, representing the hard-faced Tory landowners.'

'But of course,' said Philip, laughing, 'I've thought of all that.'

'Anyway, let me meet Horgan,' said Aylmer. 'That's the next stage.'

After dinner they walked together along the passage back to the central lobby. A figure whom he did not recognize bumped into Philip, apologized and wandered off. A rather noisy group was walking behind them. Aylmer and Philip stood aside to let them pass.

'I say, you know,' said Philip, 'an awful lot of them are drunk after dinner.'

'Aren't they just?' said Aylmer, walking along with his hand on Philip's shoulder. 'But it never did anyone any harm that I've heard of.'

29

Philip thought suddenly that Aylmer's tolerance was intolerable, but said good-bye warmly and went off to get drunk himself.

Alymer walked home, down Victoria Street to Queen Anne's Gate, where their house was. The street was quiet and moonlit. He was thinking about the Chancellor of the Exchequer, whom he disliked but in many ways admired. But the country as a whole would never quite trust him, he thought. He liked walking down Victoria Street at night, thinking about the country as a whole, and how it would never quite trust Lloyd George. A lukewarm Imperialist, he thought with mild amusement that some of his opponents in and out of the Party would be surprised to know how deep his emotional patriotism ran: but he would never tell them. Indeed he would have preferred himself that it might have been not less deep but a little less emotional, for he did believe in detachment combined with principles. 'Patriotism is the last refuge of a scoundrel,' had Dr. Johnson said? He did not much read Dr. Johnson. He must look it up.

Cynthia was not yet in. He had not expected her. He poured himself out a whisky and soda, meaning to drink it before going to bed, and when his hand was still on the syphon depression settled on him with startling suddenness, and an uneasy self-dissatisfaction. Damn Philip. Why didn't Cynthia come back?

But she did.

'And all in gold,' he said as she threw off her soft grey cloak.

'I was so bored and tired,' she said. 'And I thought you would be back by now. Maisie Ward Thomas is bringing Violet home.'

'Good. I'm glad you came. But bored and tired? You must be getting spoilt. Success has gone to your head. I'm not surprised at your success, I must admit; I do believe you get more beautiful all the time. It's nothing to do with your smart clothes and all the rest of it. Cynthia, you do know I am still the first of your admirers, don't you? Do I forget to tell you that sometimes?'

She shook her head gently. 'I wasn't really bored and tired. I came back because I felt you were sad and I wanted to be with you.'

'How did you know?' he asked.

'I felt it,' she smiled. 'I felt a deep heavy gloom coming washing towards me all the way from Victoria Street to Chester Square and I knew that it came from you. So there. Perhaps I should take up theosophy or something.'

'No, no, I want all your intuitions for myself. How wonderful.' He sat beside her and held her hand. 'I'm cured already. But it was Philip, I think, who depressed me. That and this long noisy week. He came to see me. He wants to leave the Army and put money in some stockbroking venture, but when he was talking to me I suddenly had the feeling that his motives were all wrong and he was only doing it because he resents not having enough money to cut a dash among his brother officers, and because he resents Edmund, and that made me feel that perhaps we have failed him in some way. But how?'

'What else could we have done, given the situation?' she asked.

'I don't know. He made me feel—I don't know—dull, pompous, unsympathetic, because I tried very mildly to say something of what I felt to him. But am I? Am I those things? I know I am getting older, and established in my ways, and less open to new ideas. But I haven't stopped questioning myself, have I? Do I represent something to Philip that perhaps just by being here I am? Am I authority and is authority a fake? But I am a Liberal. I am not in the other tradition at all. And besides authority, good authority, is not in the least a fake. Why should Philip make me feel this? What is it in him that I feel but don't recognize and that disturbs me so? And how ought I to deal with it?' He took her other hand as well and kissed them both. 'Now I have asked you all my questions. And immediately they have stopped bothering me.'

'It isn't like you to have so many,' she said, 'It's Philip. He does make one feel like that, standing towards him as we do. He is not reasonable, you see, as you are. But I know that you're the one who is right, absolutely right—and I know that, as you say, it's a good thing to ask yourself questions—but you know you're right too, really. I'll ask Philip to come and see me. We must see more of him. We mustn't let him grow away from us as he has been doing, at least not until we feel more confidence in him.'

'Will you? Do. He adores you, you know. You are the one person he doesn't mock.'

'Doesn't he? I wonder. But I'll try with him. I'll try harder. My dear, I think you need sleep. It's so unlike you to have a down phase that I know its tiredness more than anything. Come along.'

'May I come and undress you?'

They had separate but adjoining rooms. He came with her into hers, and undid the shining gold dress and let it slip silkily over her petticoats to lie at her feet. He brushed her long dark hair. When she was in bed he went into his own room to undress and put on his pyjamas; then he came in and lay beside her and said, 'Thank you, my darling, for being so kind.' They lay side by side. Then he kissed her. 'I am sorry for being just a gross man,' he said. 'I mean you are so eternally kind to me. If I—if I bothered you, you would tell me?'

She stroked his head and told him that he did not bother her.

Philip drunk. Philip kicking his way along a street in Soho, looking for Cindy, whose number he had forgotten. Looking in at dingy doorways, asking night people here and there, 'Cindy live here?', being brushed off, stumbling on angrily.

And then an old woman fell in his path, a heavy old woman, grey-haired, in a shapeless overcoat, carrying something; fell and grazed her cheek on the pavement, so that the heavy old veined face she raised to stare at him was spattered with blood down one side: she stared with bewildered hostility like a punch-drunk boxer without raising her head from the pavement. He stared back, swaying, welcoming her and loathing her. An old man appeared, helped her up, asked questions, took charge. Seeing Philip he told him briskly to fetch a doctor—'Doctor Simpson, end of this road, tell him to come to my place, Dick Hustler's.' Philip nodded and walked on, keeping close to the wall because he knew he was not walking steadily and did not want the old man to see. He thought determinedly of that bloodstained stupid face. They think they can wipe out ugliness by an Insurance Act . . . Cynthia's face on the pavement . . . I'm not going to mess about with any damned stupid doctors, my time's too precious . . . got to get on, find Cindy, make love, sleep . . . sleep . . . am I going to be sick? . . . let her die, the sooner the better. But the doctor's nameplate was there without his looking for it and the bell was so easily accessible and the maid answered so promptly. 'Accident . . . Dick Hustler . . . someone taken ill . . . no, no . . .' and he was off again, round the corner and across the road and up the little street he felt sure this time must be Cindy's. But why had he told the doctor, curse it? He had meant not to. Why had he meant not to? He did not know. 'Cindy live here?'

'Top floor. Mind the stairs. Light's gone.'

He remembered the stairs. Stars through the uncurtained top window. She was out. Rattle the door. It opened. She in a kimono, befringed.

'Wait a moment, can't you? I'm coming. What do you want anyway? Oh, it's you. Thought you were never coming back.'

'I wasn't.'

It was warm in her room, pleasant too, orange curtains, white walls, cushions. She was an artists' model, twenty-eight, unlucky in love, over-enthusiastic and rather ill. She said she would make some coffee. He lay on her sofa and immediately fell into a deep sleep.

In the morning he did not want to see her, and besides he had to be on parade at 11 o'clock. He left before she woke up.

Chapter Six

Cynthia had just received a declaration from a duke. She had rejected his offer of a liaison. His manner, though commendably calm in the circumstances, nevertheless betrayed enough agitation for Philip, who was shown in a few minutes after the incident, to suspect something of what had been going on. After a little polite conversation, and the most controlled and decorous of farewells, the duke left.

Philip asked, 'Is he your lover?'

Cynthia blushed. 'You are impossible, Philip.'

'Is he?'

'Of course not. Why are you always so aggressively outspoken?'

'I'm sorry.'

But she could not forgo a little jubilation. 'I must admit—but, Philip, seriously you are not to tell a soul—I must confess that something of the sort was evidently in his mind.'

'I thought as much. Did he pounce?'

'No, no, no, of course he didn't pounce. He merely—made a suggestion. No, you're not to laugh. It's not at all funny.'

'Why are you laughing yourself then? Go on. What did you say?'

'I said no of course. But really I can't help being rather amused. You see, Sylvia Newton told me last week that she was perfectly certain he had designs on her and that she couldn't make up her mind what to do about it. Poor Sylvia, I am afraid she's fallen in love with him.'

'You don't mean poor Sylvia at all. But I thought she was *afichée* with another.'

'Oh no, that was all over long ago. But really we shouldn't be talking like this.'

'Why not? Tell me, have you had many lovers?'

She was no longer amused. 'Of course not.'

'But your friends do?'

'If some of my friends have discreet adventures of one sort or another, that's no reason why I should. Did you seriously think that I did?'

'I didn't know. That's why I asked.'

'You are quite naïve in some ways although you pretend to be so blasé. One's not necessarily fast because one has some fast friends. Besides, I have some very slow ones as well.'

'Will you tell Aylmer about the duke?'

'I don't know. Perhaps not. It would look like boasting.'

'Weren't you boasting to me just now?'

'It doesn't matter boasting to you. Besides, it had only that moment happened. If you had come in half an hour later I shouldn't have boasted even to you.'

'I suppose people often make this sort of proposition to you. Is it true that the late king did?'

'Of course not. How can I stop you asking these impertinent questions? Really, you have no right to do it. If you go on I shall be as angry as I ought to be already.'

'I was awfully in love with you myself when I was eight.'

'That was a long time ago and gives you no right to cross-examine me now.'

'Do you remember that time, when I first came?'

'I remember that you kept hitting me all the time.'

'That was because I was in love with you.'

'It seems an odd form for love to take. You were dreadfully difficult.'

'That was because I was in love with you. I was. I had never seen anyone like you before. Everyone in India was either Indian or yellow. There was no one as white as you, no one with those white shoulders, no one who wore such clothes, or laughed like you, or was so soft.'

'And so you hit me?'

'And so I hit you. Don't you believe in my great love?'

'Of course,' She walked over to ring the bell for tea. 'It is very touching. When did you grow out of it?'

'Perhaps I never did.'

'That serves me right for asking such a stupid question. At least you don't hit me any more. Now let's talk about something else. I hear you have decided to send in your papers.'

'Yes. Aylmer doesn't approve.'

'He told me he did.'

'Did he? Tell me what he said.'

'That he approved.'

'And what else?'

'Now you are rapping questions at me again. I won't have it. Sit down and have some tea.'

A silver tea tray having just been brought in, she poured some out and went on, 'Aylmer thinks it's a good idea because he wants you to do something which you yourself believe to be worth while. That's all, nothing more complicated. And he will meet Mr. Hogan with an unprejudiced mind.'

'Horgan. Yes, I know he will. And listen carefully. And sum the whole thing up with exquisite precision at the end. And advise a cautious advance. And provide the money. And be helpful in every way.'

'Then what more can you possibly want?'

'What indeed?'

'Then what is wrong? Explain yourself.'

'I can't. Does Aylmer like me?'

'Like you? Don't be absurd. He loves you. We look on you as our son.'

'I feel that I can't somehow reach him, or shake him. I should like to shake him.'

'How violent you are. You hit people you love and want to shake your truly loving and devoted uncle. What is the matter with you?'

'Nothing. I am very happy, as a matter of fact, at this moment. Aren't you?'

'Happy? Yes. But then I often am.'

'I feel much more as if it were you and I who were of the same blood, don't you? And yet we are hardly related at all.'

'We are. I am your aunt by marriage and your adoptive mother.'

'Yes, Aunt Cynthia. And don't you sometimes feel a bond with me closer than that one?'

'No. I think that is a very close one.'

'No, but—sometimes I feel that with you there are no barriers. You are almost the only person with whom I do feel this. And yet I have a lot of secrets from you. And you, I suppose, from me.'

'I have hardly any secrets from anybody.'

'Why aren't we always like this, though? Why do we sometimes quarrel and why do you irritate me so? I suppose it is when you are being Aylmerish.'

'Philip, I cannot let you say one word against Aylmer.'

'I am not saying anything against Aylmer. You know I never would. I am only saying that some of his qualities don't exactly suit you. At least they do suit you in a way, I suppose, but not to my mind. To my mind they veil your splendour. Tell me—just because at this moment we *are* close, you know we are—haven't you ever wanted them, any of the others?'

'If you mean lovers, no, I have never wanted them. Do sit down and stop fidgeting.'

'I was bringing my cup for some more tea.'

'Why don't we talk about your affairs? Why you don't get married for instance. After all, you're twenty-eight.'

'How old are you?'

'Forty-one. But I don't like thinking about it.'

'Are you afraid of getting old, of your beauty going, of wanting things you haven't had when it's too late to have them?'

'No. And we are talking about you, not me.'

'I don't get married because I have no money.'

'You have a little. And I expect Aylmer would try to give you a little more if you married. Besides, you are going to make a fortune.'

'Then I don't marry because none of the girls I meet are as beautiful as you. They are all little skimpy creatures with no bosoms.'

She burst out laughing. 'Philip, I will not sit here drinking tea and talking about bosoms. You are too disgraceful. I insist on talking about the latest play.'

'I never go to the theatre. It bores me.'

'Well then, the latest book.'

'I don't read either.'

'Anyway here's Aylmer. Now you'll have to behave.'

'I'll have to run as well. It's later than I thought. How could you have kept me dallying here like this? I'm on duty at 6 o'clock.'

She gave him her hand and said, 'Come and see me again.'

She heard him talking briefly in the hall with Aylmer. Then the door banged and Aylmer came in.

'Philip seemed cheerful,' he said.

'He was,' She rose to kiss him on the cheek. 'I don't think we need worry about him. He doesn't mean half he says, you know. And he is so sweet when he is being nice. I am so glad you are coming with me this evening. It's going to be fun, I know. I shall wear my black velvet and all my diamonds and everyone will be amazed at me. Don't you think so? And I shall be frivolous and flirtatious and everything reprehensible and you will be quite ashamed of me.'

'I dare say. And in the meantime I should like some tea.'

And here she is in her black velvet and all her diamonds, pausing at the top of the stairs which lead, so conveniently for dramatic effect, down into the crowded

37

reception-room. And the faces turn, obediently. And she pauses, pretending to look for her hostess, turning her head with its elaborate gleaming pile of hair first to one side then to the other, on the famous long white neck. And how gloriously white the shoulders and the bosom, how fine the moulding of the arms, how wide the great dark gaze of the eyes. But the pause is not a moment too long. She begins to move, and Aylmer, happy in his role, follows a step or two behind, and she glides down the stairs with the velvet spreading out behind her, and her smile begins slowly and widens for her hostess, and she stretches out both jewelled hands, as it were impulsively, and what a benefit she bestows!

And later an ambassador says, 'I must tell you that I think you make the most beautiful entrances,' and is quite ravished by the serene happiness of the smile with which she answers, *'Don't* I?'

Chapter Seven

The girls in the Gothic summer-house were talking about love: it was all very suitable. They wore their morning clothes, Alice a long blue skirt, tightly belted, and a striped blouse with a short tie, Kitty a white muslin dress and long black stockings: they had been carrying hats. The summer-house was in the wood, well placed in a sunny clearing overlooking the narrow valley. They had walked across two fields and through a wicket gate to reach it and, though Kitty was holding a book which she was supposed to be reading aloud (they were doing Ruskin), they felt themselves far enough from the intimidating influence of old Mrs. Weston to neglect their studies. Kitty was envying Alice for having had the unhappy love affair to which she had at last admitted.

'Then of course you will never marry,' said Kitty. 'You will devote your life to lost causes. Have you ever thought of becoming a nun?'

'I don't think I should care for it,' said Alice. 'And the truth is not so much that I shall never marry as that no one will ever marry me. Everyone knows, you see, at home, so of course no man in his right mind would have anything to do with me.'

'No, of course not,' said Kitty. 'It would be all right if you were a widow. But anyway you can't want to marry, surely? I mean, you will never love again, will you?'

'Oh dear, I don't think it's as romantic as that. I didn't love so very much then anyway. I mean that I—I was attracted and I admired him and . . . but love doesn't really begin until it is returned. At least that's what I think. And this was not returned, so it amounted to nothing.'

'But it must have been returned a little?'

'He was flirting,' said Alice firmly. 'He liked going for walks with me and holding my hand and—that sort of thing—and then he married someone else.'

'Beast,' said Kitty. 'I hate men anyway. I shan't marry. I'm going to go about teaching the poor about birth-control. You can come with me if you like.'

'Oh Kitty, for heaven's sake. . . !'

'Why not? These poor women get absolutely worn out with childbirth. It's quite disgraceful. Just because the men come home drunk on Friday nights and wreak their filthy passions on them. Well, they do. Why are you laughing?'

'I'm not. I mean. I know there is something in it, but, oh dear . . . and then anyway don't you think it might not be so simple as that? Perhaps the women sometimes like it?'

'Like having babies? Oh you mean like . . . ? Good heavens, no, that's quite impossible. Well, really, Alice it is. No one could possibly enjoy it. I know, because I've read about it in the medical dictionary and it must be simply revolting.'

'Hush! Someone's coming.'

Kitty picked up the book and began to read at a rattling pace: '. . . but most of our great teachers, not excepting Carlyle and Emerson themselves, are a little too encouraging in their proclamation of this comfort, not to my mind very sufficient, when for the present our fields are full of nothing but darnel instead of wheat, and cockle instead of barley; and none of them seem to me yet to have enough insisted on the inevitable power and infectiousness of all evil, and the easy and utter extinguishableness of good. Medicine often fails of its effect, but poison never; and while, in summing up . . .' But looking up she burst out laughing, because it was Edmund, and she could see from his face that he knew she had only just picked up the book.

He had carried out his plan to come down to Charleswood and work in peace for his examinations and had already been there for some days. He persuaded them now to come with him for a walk, saying that it was so late in the morning that it would be better to leave Ruskin for after lunch.

Old Mrs. Weston was on her way back from the village in her car, driven by her chauffeur Ralph Moberley. She lived in a certain style at Charleswood, with her own rooms at the top of the house, her own maid, Fletcher, whom she loathed, and Moberley and the Silver Wraith, to both of whom she was devoted. The Silver Wraith had a glass screen between driver and passenger, and a speaking tube. When she was bored, which was quite often, she would send for the car and Moberley, and they would drive about the countryside, talking on the speaking tube. The idea of sending for Moberley and talking to him without the intercession of the speaking tube, which would have saved her many meaningless journeys and pointless calls, would never have occurred to her.

Today he was driving her back from the village, where she had been to see old Mrs. Maidment and taken her some meat jelly. Mrs. Maidment lived in the almshouses and was probably dying. She was not yet as old as Mrs. Weston, but she had lost her memory, so that she still sewed buttons on to her husband's shirts, and sometimes got his tea ready for him, though he had been dead three years.

'I believe that in some primitive tribes,' said old Mrs. Weston down the tube, 'they kill off the old people as soon as they become a burden to the community. I dare say there's something in it.'

'As long as they're not a burden to themselves,' said Moberley.

'You think they should be allowed to survive until they become that?'

'I think everybody should be allowed to live out the term of their natural life,' said Moberley firmly. 'But it's when they become a burden to themselves that you can't help wishing their natural life might come to this end. Like Mrs. Maidment there.'

'How's Beatrice?'

'Much the same, thank you, 'm.'

'Still pressing you?'

He smiled. He was rather handsome.

'You're mad if you do it.'

'I want a good wife, that's all. Not one of these flighty creatures. You don't know what they're up to the minute you turn your back.'

'She's got a mean mouth.'

'A good head, though. I need someone with a strong character. I'm weak myself. That's always been my trouble.'

'You're not in the least weak. It's just that Beatrice is much cleverer than you. What you want is a nice cheerful wife like little Ellen.'

He did not answer.

'You like her don't you?' persisted Mrs. Weston interferingly.

'Well, I do, yes 'm. But you see the trouble is, I'm afraid she's one of the flighty ones like I was saying. And I've seen where that can lead. I don't want that sort of trouble.'

'She'd settle down. Does she like you?'

'I think she does. But you see there was a baker. A year ago it was all the baker. Then he went off, married a girl from somewhere near Marlborough, went to live there, I believe, and that was the end of that.'

'What bad luck. No doubt he misled her. We'll go on a little bit, drive about. Mrs. Maidment has depressed me. My life is pointless. All I can do is interfere in your affairs and prepare myself for death. Do you realize that? I am prepared for death, too, sometimes. Prepared to embrace it. But not always, not when I have been with Mrs. Maidment. Do you believe in God, Moberley?'

'I do, 'm.'

'Do you find it difficult to sustain that belief?'

'No, 'm, I can't say I do. Anything else would be terrible to me.'

'It is terrible,' said old Mrs. Weston. 'You are quite right. And quite right to stick to it. Sometimes I despair. My definition of despair is recognition of one's own incapacity to create God. I can create Him sometimes. When I can't I despair. It is the worst sin I know, worse than anything poor little Ellen did with the baker. If she did do anything.'

'That's it, you see, that's the problem,' said Moberley gloomily.

'But you receive Him ready made at the hands of others. In their own image. What if they should let you down?'

'They won't do that, 'm,' he said reassuringly, though not at all clear as to what she might be trying to say.

'If she is fond of you I think you should forgive her her adventure with the baker. I think you would do well together.'

'That's what I tell myself sometimes, but the trouble is it's not so simple as that. I mean, it's a fundamental thing in a man, isn't it? And Beatrice, whatever her faults, is a good woman.'

'She thinks she is, anyway. I dare say she has many good qualities—endurance for instance, and reliability—but the other is such an affectionate sweet-natured creature. Ah well, you're in a lucky situation. But don't let Beatrice bully you into anything. I shouldn't be in a hurry at all if I were you.'

'I shan't rush into anything, 'm. I've never been impetuous.'

'And you won't commit yourself finally without discussing it with me? It helps to talk about it, you know. I don't expect you to take my advice.'

'I certainly value it very highly, 'm.'

'I feel better now. We can go home, if you please. She's going well, isn't she? You found out what the trouble was the other day, I see. Was it the plugs?'

They discussed the engine all the way home. Old Mrs. Weston liked the technical details.

Alice writing home again: . . . He has lent me a book called *Principia Ethica* by a certain G.E. Moore. Does Father know about him? Edmund knows him and admires him very much. The point of the whole thing seems to be that the highest values in life are those involved in human relations and the appreciation of beauty—and all one has to do is to deal with those beautifully. Now that I come to think of it, it seems an awfully long and difficult book to say just that, so I expect I have not got it quite right—I must read the book to find the subtleties, but it sounds nice, doesn't it, and so entirely right a philosophy for a character like Edmund's? He is such a fortunate person and so nicely aware of it that it is delightful to be with him (no, I am *not* with him too much, and I do *not* over-reach myself in any way, and my bearing is *everything* that is proper for a person in my position). At Whitsun the house is going to be full—they have all asked people to stay—Kitty says it will be ghastly, nothing but *games*—but I am sure to be entranced, and after that she and I are to have a week in London to be spent in improving activities. Please will Father send me a list of things I should take her to see, apart from obvious ones like the National Gallery?'

Chapter Eight

The Guards' Club. Captain Smallpiece in the smoking-room, his feet up, snoring slightly over the *Field*. They are small feet, spankingly shod by Lobb: the whole small form in the armchair is neat as anything; even the head, though it lolls, has carefully brushed hair and a carefully trimmed moustache (by Trumper). Captain Smallpiece is Captain Weston's best friend in the regiment—in fact almost his only friend. He finds old Philip an amusing chap and besides, he says, the Westons are all right—there was old Charlie Weston who used to be in the regiment and old Gummy Weston in the Blues and old Hugo Weston who was sacked from Eton and became a general, and Aylmer Weston's said to be a very decent fellow and awfully brilliant and all that— so that when Philip sits suddenly down beside him he opens his slightly bulging eyes obligingly (revealing himself to be a good deal younger than one might have supposed) and hardly reproaches him for waking him, merely murmuring, 'What? What?' with mild irritation.

'Sorry. Did I make you jump? Take a few deep breaths. Want a drink?'

'Wouldn't mind some more of that port, it's not half bad. How'd you get on?'

'Exactly as I expected to. Aylmer was charming. Horgan duly bowled over. Aylmer did a bit of his usual lightning grasp stuff, which went down pretty well. Horgan on the other hand was quite tough and business-like and refused to be overawed. The only person who came out of it badly was me.'

'What happened? Get a bit squiffy?'

'Wish I had. No. Just general ineptitude. Furious with Aylmer for being patronizing, furious with Horgan for being so common and awful.'

'What is he? Jew, I imagine?'

'Just South African.'

'Course he's a Jew. All South Africans are Jews. Can't think why you go on with it if you don't care for the fellow. Far better stick to this sort of life, hunt with your own pack, don't you know?'

'It's all very well for you. You're rich, apart from anything else.'

'Don't know about that. Income tax going up all the time. And death duties. If your uncle's Party stays in power much longer there's no knowing what will become of hereditary wealth.'

'And a good thing too. There's going to be a great upheaval. There's a whole new force coming up, based on everything that's been suppressed up till now, based on bad taste if you like. A whole new wave and I'm on the crest of it.'

'I can see that it might appeal to you. Still, rather you than me. Going in there, meeting the Jews on their own ground, damned courageous thing to do if you ask me.'

'But there's money in it, Buffy. And anyway that sort of thing's not going to matter any more, being a Jew I mean. Class barriers are going to break down and in the process there'll be gains to be made. Gains, Buffy.'

'Not a question of class really I'd have said. I mean a Jew's a Jew, isn't he, not some sort of damned middle-class muck? A Jew's a Jew. And proud of it I daresay. More a question of race really, isn't it? And you can't tell me race barriers are going to break down. What I mean to say is, a Jew's a Jew and a black's a black and an Englishman's an Englishman, and more power to their elbow, I say, all of them. And I know which I'd rather be. Yes, well, anyway, I dare say I'd look a pretty good ass as a

44

black fellow. Haven't got the physique, sort of thing. All that naked dancing. So you think power is slipping from the hands of the hereditary ruling classes, is that it? Good God, what a frightful thing.'

'Is it?'

'Of course it is. Well, I mean, who's going to take over? Who's got the experience? The sense of responsibility?'

'I don't know. Who cares, so long as there's a change, a chance for a bit of real life to creep in?'

'I suppose you want the middle classes to take over. God, how dreary. Let's get that over as quick as possible and get the working classes in. At least they like gin. Sort of thing. Or am I quite wrong? I dare say I am. But what I mean is, what's wrong with the present chaps?'

'They're corrupt, inefficient, money-mad, immoral, unjust, based on falsehood. Their whole creed's a pack of lies.'

'Oh lor'. But look here, what about your uncle? You can't say all those things about him. I mean he's a bit of a rebel, a bit of a revolutionary idealistic kind of dangerous politician, but no one's ever said there was anything wrong with his motives.'

'He's the worst of the lot. The worst of the lot. He pretends to understand, he ought to, he thinks he does, but he doesn't.'

'Really? Oh dear. How rotten. Thought he was a good chap.'

'Oh he's a good chap. And I'll make him suffer for it.'

'What's wrong with being a good chap?'

'Nothing. As long as he doesn't discount the bad chaps. And the bad chap in him.'

'Oh you mean Aylmer's got another side to him. Vice and all that. Really? What bad luck. Look here, what about a game of backgammon?'

'All right. I shall beat you, though.'

'I know. You always do. We might have another glass of that port, don't you think?'

Chapter Nine

At Whitsun the house was full of people. I haven't described the house because I know it too well, as one cannot describe one's mother's face. But if ever you have had dreams of a beautiful house they were dreams of Charleswood.

And I can't remember the names of the people who stayed there for those two weeks, it was too long ago; and if I looked them up in those now tattered scrap-books they all used to keep with photographs and private jokes and mottoes grandly though illegibly signed, I should only become muddled. My memory would be jolted uncomfortably by finding that Margaret James wasn't after all the one who flirted with Philip; she was the one with dark hair who later married John Abinger, and it was Margaret Pope Fairfax who was the flirt and Cicely was not Cicely Anderson but Cicely Carmichael, and it was Mildred Anderson whose cousin Hubert later married Cicely only the day before he left for France in 1915. And then, as I say, I should be muddled and remember the whole thing less clearly than I do now. Because it doesn't really matter if I get their names wrong; we know that Violet and Wilfred were there, and Edmund and Philip and Alice and Kitty; and there was also Margaret, and Joan and Daisy and Ida and Cicely, and Robin and Gerald and the two Johns. Perhaps they were not all staying at the same time but came and went during the two weeks. A lot of them were there the day they played hide-and-seek while Aylmer worked in the library and Cynthia sat with her sewing in the shade and watched them. There are, of course, plenty of people alive now who were grown up then. But not these.

I think it was Cicely who suggested playing hide-and-seek. They were all out in the garden saying it was too hot to play tennis, suggesting croquet, a group walking off towards the wood, another sitting on the grass under the cedar-tree continuing a conversation they had begun at lunch. Edmund and John said they would play a single in spite of the heat, Cicely, who was not much good at tennis and had hoped for a walk with Edmund, was disap-

46

pointed, knowing that Edmund was likely to go on playing tennis all afternoon if once he started, and so she said, 'Let's play hide-and-seek—this would be a wonderful place for it,' and Violet, who was all that time in a state of mild delirium brought on by the excitement of her engagement, jumped up and said, 'I'll hide!' and ran across the lawn towards the orangery, disappearing in a moment behind the Portugal laurels; but Wilfred and John ran after her and it turned into a game of 'touch', and Cicely and Ida joined in and they ran round and round the small formal rose-garden in front of the orangery, jumping the low box hedges, until Ida fell by the fountain and one of her feet slipped into the pool, so she took off her shoes and stockings; but by that time the others had all joined them and they went into the orangery to talk to the cockatoo who was 100 years old, but soon came out because Mason, the head gardener, was in there watering and they knew he was cross with them for having raided his greenhouse the day before and stolen peaches. Ida stayed behind to soothe him. Her hair was dark gold, her eyes sometimes green sometimes grey, she was tall, and nineteen; perhaps she had let her foot slip into the fountain on purpose, because she liked being barefoot: it was always she who after they had danced all night and had evaded the chaperons to escape into the garden was the first to throw off her shoes and stockings and run barefoot across the dewy lawn.

'He is subjugated,' said Ida, having dealt with Mason, 'but I am still frowned on by your grandmother. I shall put on my best Sunday hat and walk up and down the terrace reading Schopenhauer.'

'No, come with me and hide. The others must find us. They must count 200 first. I have got my Yeats; we can sit in an arbour and read verses till they find us.' Cicely, long-faced, soft-voiced, subject to sweeping enthusiasms.

Ida pretended to be an old Irish peasant woman. 'The years like great black oxen tread on the floor of time, and I am broken by their passing feet.'

'To me, fair friend, you never can be old, for as you were when first your eye I eyed . . .'

'We must all sit here until we have made a sonnet with two puns in it, then we will come and find you.'

47

'That will be too long.'

'Not clever games in the afternoons as well as in the evenings?'

'Clumps is not clever.'

'Nor is cock-fighting. Let's make your father play again this evening.'

'If we were going to play hide-and-seek Kitty must play too. Where is she?'

'Reading with Alice.'

'Tell them both to come. Go on, you two, hide. We'll paddle in the fountain until you're ready.'

So all afternoon they wandered in the garden, looking for each other; and some were found quickly and some more slowly, and some took the seeking seriously and some simply walked and talked; and Kitty when it was her turn to hide climbed a tree, and Gerald found her and climbed higher and then they all began to climb trees, but Kitty wanted to hide again and so they played 'sardines' until only Daisy wandered with her sweet blurred mermaid look between the rose-strewn trees, not knowing they were all in the hayloft waiting for her. They had to give it away in the end by singing the Pilgrims' Chorus from *Tannhäuser* louder and louder until she heard them; and then it was Alice's turn to hide. She came back towards the house and hid behind a weeping ash. Cynthia could see her from where she sat sewing. For a long time there was no one else to be seen. They had all scattered farther afield. Then Philip appeared, walking slowly, his hands in the pockets of his white flannel trousers. He was looking in the wrong direction. He did not seem particularly interested in the game. Cynthia thought, Perhaps he will come and sit beside me, and talk? But suddenly he changed direction, walked towards the ash, and round it, and discovered Alice. They stood together, hiding from the others. But the others were nowhere to be seen. It seemed a long time that Cynthia watched them standing close together, talking in whispers. How could the others be so stupid? Perhaps they had given up, decided to do something different, gone for a walk or a bicycle ride. Then at the other end of the lawn Edmund and Cicely appeared, but they walked so slowly, and the whispered conversation behind the ash seemed to be growing more and more engrossing. Cynthia almost called out to

Edmund, almost called to Philip, 'They are coming', almost stood up herself so that Alice and Philip might realize she could see them. But it was too late. He had kissed her. He had bent his head and kissed her on the cheek.

It would have been better if she could have spoken to them about it or to Alice anyway, for Philip might have teased her (he had known that she could see them), but Alice would probably have been able to set her mind at rest by showing how little the incident had meant to her and how much more worrying to her was the idea that she might have incurred Cynthia's displeasure.

Nor did Cynthia mention the incident to Aylmer. He did not like unpleasantness.

She sent for Alice and said, 'I am a little worried about Kitty. Of course when there is a young party here she wants to join in, but we mustn't forget that she is supposed to be still in the schoolroom. She will have time enough for social life when she is out. I do want her to pursue her studies seriously while she can.'

'Yes, of course.'

'I think it is so important for a woman to have the balance that a good education can give, quite apart from the pleasure it will give to herself and to others. But you know how we feel about it. I think it would be better if in the afternoons you and she kept yourselves to the schoolroom.'

Alice flushed slightly. 'I did feel when Miss Weston came up yesterday to ask us to play hide-and-seek that I ought to have asked you first, but she said that it was a holiday and there was no need—but of course I should have asked all the same—I am so sorry. Kitty is getting on very well. She has such an eager and inquiring mind I don't think she will ever stop educating herself. She is really a joy to teach.'

'I have heard about your progress from my mother-in-law and I am very pleased that it is all going so well. It is just that I don't want it to relax now that the house is full, and now that there are going to be other distractions because of the wedding. I don't want Kitty to become purely frivolous like some girls of her age.'

'No indeed.'

Alice understood that this meant that the governess was not to join in too readily with the fun of the house party.

She in no way resented the mild rebuke but wished only that she had done nothing to deserve it.

To Philip Cynthia said nothing at all. Even when he said quite openly when they were walking together down towards the tennis court, 'I am thinking of having a little flirtation with the governess,' she turned to him a face of only mild reproach and said, 'Is that kind?'

'To whom?'

'To the governess.'

'Oh, I can't be expected to consider *her* feelings.'

'And I can't be expected to take *you* seriously. Will you join me in a plot to foil Edmund of his design to play six sets running before tea? He does it so subtly that people don't notice until too late that he has organized himself into every four.'

'I will join you in any plot you care to propose to me.'

'Then I must think of a really dashing one.'

She ascribed the strength of the emotion she concealed to a desire like Aylmer's to 'avoid unpleasantness'. She told herself that Philip's behaviour was disappointing and unworthy of him. She was afraid that Alice might be turning out to be 'light'. When she looked at the governess's clear fine-eyed face and saw the suitable unflustered politeness with which in public she replied to Philip's conversational openings—or to anyone else's—she was half comforted, but half even more disquieted in case this was just a cool cover for a secret intrigue.

'You seem restless,' Aylmer said to her one evening. He had come into her bedroom as she was about to change for tea and found her walking up and down in front of the windows. 'Is anything the matter? You are not letting this wedding get on your mind, are you?'

'No, it is nothing.' She stood with her back to him, looking out of the window. 'It is pretty. I mean, I like to see them in the garden, in the sun. Ida is lovely, isn't she? They all are. But sometimes I am afraid that underneath it all there might be something less agreeable.'

'You, the ever-sanguine?' He stood beside her, looking down into the garden. A group was walking up from the tennis court, Violet and Wilfred were sitting under the cedar with Margaret, Ida and John were walking towards them talking. Ida animated and gesticulating. 'They're all right,' he said.

She turned away rather sharply and said, 'Of course they are. I must dress. Aren't they coming in to change? They'll be late. I'm not going to wear that silly pink thing. I can't think why Beatrice has put it out. I'll wear the green one.'

Aylmer rang for Beatrice. 'I see the village girl guides have sent Violet a hatpin stand.'

'Yes, a hideous one. They really might have done better.'

'But it was good of them to make such an effort.'

'They seem to think Kitty is going to take over the running of them now. I can't imagine she will be any good at it. She's hopelessly irresponsible.'

'I think she's improving under Miss Benedict.'

'Oh, Miss Benedict. Why does nobody ever stop singing her praises? I don't believe she's as wonderful as all that anyway. Oh Beatrice, I'll wear my green, not that pink horror.'

'I'll go down then.' Aylmer went to the door and added, with a look of vague anxiety, before he left, 'Don't worry, will you?'

She did not answer.

Philip had become aware of something else.

After he had kissed Alice, she stood quite still for a moment, because she had been taken by surprise. They had been talking about the people staying in the house and Alice had been praising the beauty of the girls, and he, close to her because they were hiding, had said, 'I don't think any of them are as pretty as you,' and kissed her on the cheek. After a moment she moved away from him and said calmly, 'I can hardly think you mean that.' And then they heard Cicely's voice, and then they were discovered. But she was slightly flushed, her expression not as carefree as it should have been, and Edmund, knowing Philip, guessed what might have happened and thought, Blast Philip, looking at her face with attention. It seemed to him that she returned him a look not of confusion but of trust, so he immediately placed himself between her and Philip (since they were all in a close group, hiding) and began a whispered conversation about the progress of the game.

Philip, annoyed by her reaction, noticed Edmund's too and thought, So he's not uninterested either—that's a

51

joke, with all these eligible girls about—an entanglement with the governess—that would give them something to think about. It gave, of course, more point to his own pursuit, but that, he had to admit, did not for the moment seem to be progressing very rapidly.

Under the cedar tree they were talking about statues, about what they would all represent if they were to be turned then and there to stone. Ida was to be Youth, Wilfred Fortitude, Violet Spring; someone suggested Retribution for old Mrs. Weston, and Truth for Cynthia.

'No, Beauty, of course.'

'Day.'

'Beauty is Truth, Truth Beauty.'

'The Ideal,' said Ida.

'Eve,' said Philip.

'No, I don't want her to be Eve,' said Ida. 'Adam didn't love her.'

'Oh surely . . . ?'

'No, no, he didn't love her. If he had loved her he would never have sneaked to God in the way he did. He treated her very shabbily.'

'But she had rather ruined everything.'

'He had eaten the apple too, even if she had done it first. And his love should have been stronger—she had not changed. His reaction was selfish, only thinking of his own injury and not of hers through the serpent. But perhaps if he had loved enough he would not even have blamed the serpent. Then they could have had their own Paradise in spite of God.'

'With the serpent in it?'

'Yes, with the serpent. They could have made allowances for the serpent.'

'I think you ask too much of Adam.'

'Of course. That's the whole point. So she must not be Eve.'

'All right then, let her be Life. Or the Ideal, as you said. What we all dream that Life might be.'

'But that makes her different to each of us.'

'Oh no, we all have the same ideal. She shall be the Ideal. And Sir Aylmer Learning.'

'No, Goodwill.'

'Philip should be Darkness, the Unknown.'

'Or Violence. Edmund should be Hope.'

Cynthia herself had wandered away from them before the conversation began. She was picking roses. Between her face and a white rose she saw Philip's dark head, bending. 'Oh no!' she cried.

'Have you pricked yourself?' Old Mrs. Weston was on her way back to the house with a basket of young dandelion leaves. She made them into rather bitter salads for herself alone.

'No, it is nothing,' said Cynthia.

'If you are feeling like that, it is important to keep warm and eat well,' said old Mrs. Weston, detached.

Chapter Ten

Parliament reassembled on 9th June. The following week Kitty and Alice went to London. Aylmer gave them lunch at the House of Commons, and afterwards they listened to the debate. He was very busy at that time: it was going to be a harassing session. Ireland and the militant women were the problems. Here we have *The Times* of 9th June on the question of the women, begging the Government to take some action in view of the danger of private citizens taking the matter into their own hands: 'Instead of intimidating anybody they (the militant women) are arousing an ugly determination to pay them back in their own coin.' On the subject of Ireland *The Times* of the day before blames Ministers for not taking advantage of the recess to inform themselves at first hand of the situation there and abjures them to 'address themselves honestly to the facts of the most perilous situation which has confronted the Empire in our time'.

The Conservatives were harrying the Government. Aylmer was in favour of a General Election in the autumn, believing that the Opposition's extremist tactics over the Irish situation might lose them support in the country, but the Prime Minister wanted to reach some sort of settlement, however temporary, of the Irish problem and go to the country early the following year. As to the danger of civil war in Ireland, Aylmer was unable to believe that it could be a serious possibility. He saw the whole thing as resting simply on the drawing of an appropriate boundary between North and South—his own Party having agreed that Ulster should be excluded from Home Rule—and the deciding upon how or when Ulster should vote itself out or in; and he could not believe those problems to be insuperable, in spite of gloomy forecasts on every side. He spoke briefly in a debate on the adjournment on 17th June.

He had not meant to speak, but he had been irritated by the previous speakers, who were Bonar Law and Carson; and he also had it in mind that if an election were approaching he might do well to show himself as a more vigorous defender of his Party's policies than he too often appeared.

He referred to the Archbishop of York's recent appeal to Members of Parliament and quoted from it: 'The difficulty lies not so much in the problem itself as in the spirit in which it seems to be approached.'

Aylmer was not an outstanding speaker, though he appeared to better advantage in the House of Commons than on the platform. He had a pleasant light voice which carried well and an agreeably reasonable air. In spite of this he found it much more difficult to put his whole point of view in a speech than at a committee meeting, and he had never been known as a keen debater.

'Who can deny,' he said, of his quotation from the Archbishop's letter, 'the truth of this observation? A year ago it was a different matter; the points of view held by the opposing Parties were harder then to reconcile. But what is the situation now? It has been agreed—it has been agreed—that special terms are to be given to Ulster, that these special terms shall be negotiated as soon as possible, and that Ulster shall have the right to make up her own mind as to her position. The hon. Member for Bootle adds at the end of his speech a brief acknowledgement of this fact—in passing he mentions it and says that in that case we shall avoid the evils on which he has been expatiating.' ('I said the worst of the evils,' said Bonar Law loudly.) 'The worst of the evils. But does this fact, this legitimate hope, in any way alter the tone, too long familiar to us all, of the rest of his speech? Not in the least. The one certain fact which seems to have emerged from the whole recent history of this controversy is the irresponsibility of His

Majesty's Opposition, who even now when the end might appear to be in sight reiterate the wild charges against the Government and their foolhardy undertakings to the inhabitants of Ulster. This spectacle of a great political Party, supposed to be seriously considered by the people of this country as an alternative Government, turning themselves for reasons of Party pride and revenge into a Party whose policy, whose considered policy, in the event of the Home Rule Bill being put into force, is one of armed rebellion against His Majesty's Government—this is a sorry spectacle. It seems to me now that it is the honour of Parliament itself which is at stake. On the ministerial side we have shown ourselves anxious only for an equable settlement—the Parliamentary Nationalist leaders are anxious for a settlement—the whole country desires it—we are approaching it, we are moving towards it—but there are still people who by their every word and action do their best to prevent it. They have no alternative to suggest to the settlement which we are seeking—their aim is a purely destructive one. They accuse us of trying to coerce the Ulster Unionists. In the same breath they attack us for not having put down by force the Ulster Volunteers. The Chief Secretary has pointed out that the whole history of Anglo-Irish relations shows the error of forcible suppression by this country. What is this military fever which has seized the Conservative Party? What is this urge towards precipitate action? "Attack, attack," they cry, these devotees of action for its own sake—but we must resist this rash appeal as men of sober and mature judgment have always tried to resist it down the centuries. We do not intend to use coercion in Ireland. We do not even intend, despite the provocation, to take up arms against His Majesty's Opposition. We intend to pursue a policy of peaceful negotiation, and I feel that we have a right at this juncture, in a situation whose gravity we must not attempt to minimize, to call upon hon. Members opposite as well as those of conflicting opinions in Ireland itself to make a serious and constructive attempt to allow an atmosphere to develop in which these negotiations may go forward with some hope of success.

'I refer again to the Archbishop's letter. "The country expects," he says, "the country expects Parliament to achieve a solution". Mr. Speaker, Sir, are we in this House going to allow Party faction, lust for Party battle for its own sake, lust for Party power, for Party revenge, to cheat the country of the fulfilment of its just and proper expectations?'

This speech was to a certain extent and among other things responsible for his being asked a few weeks later when the King made his own appeal for reason and moderation, to take part in the Buckingham Palace Conference. 'I'd like Weston to be there,' his sovereign said. 'He's a man I trust, and a patient man too.' And to this the Prime Minister, who also trusted him, agreed. But by the end of July it was too late.

It was the day after this speech that Kitty and Alice came to lunch with Aylmer. He showed them round, took pleasure in explaining various details of procedure to them, and left them in the Strangers' Gallery to listen to the debate. They did not stay long because Edmund had asked them to tea in his chambers in the Temple.

As they came out of St. Stephen's entrance they saw a young woman chained to the railings. Two policemen were attempting to unchain and remove her. She was fighting hard, kicking and clawing and screaming. Her hair was half unpinned, her face white and her large bulging eyes red-rimmed and desperate. She looked extremely ill.

Kitty rushed up to the two policemen. 'Let her go! Let her go! Oh, how can you?'

'Kitty!' Alice hurried after her and took her by the arm.

'Keep out of this,' said the policeman. 'Go on, you, get her away from here.'

'Come on, Kitty.' Alice pulled her arm.

'No, no!' Kitty resisted. They were so near that they could smell the woman. She smelt of sweat and sickness.

The woman shouted to Kitty. 'Hit him! Hit him! Go on, do something.'

'Kitty!'

'I will. I will.' Red-faced, Kitty lifted both her fists and jerked nervously in the direction of one of the policemen.

'Go along now or we'll take you with us. Get her out of the way, will you? Can't you see we've got enough on our hands?'

They had managed to detach the suffragette from the railing, and now bundled her with a good deal of vindictive pushing and pinching into a police van.

'Help me! Help me! Fight them!' she shrieked before they closed the door. Her wild face appeared mouthing at the little back window as the van drove off.

'We must do something. Why didn't you let me? How could you stand there and let those two brutes push her about and not help her? How could you?'

'Kitty, for heaven's sake let's walk along a little bit. It's not fair to your father to stand here quarrelling and shouting. Of course I felt sorry for that poor woman, but she had after all started it, she was . . .'

'She was right. She had right on her side. It's quite monstrous that they won't give women the vote. In the face of tyranny you have to use violence. Oh why didn't I do anything? Why did you stop me?'

'Because you were making a complete idiot of yourself, you know perfectly well you were. And you are quite quite wrong. There is no need at all for them to use violence—and if the policemen were brutes so was she—she had made herself one . . .'

'She had not. How can you be so unfeeling about someone who ought to be your own sister? I am very very disappointed in you, Alice.' Kitty was standing still again. They confronted each other on the pavement in Parliament Square.

'I am disappointed in you, too, for being so stupid. It is innocent people like you who cause half the trouble. What do you think human nature is that we can afford to play about with it like this? Do you think human beings are angels? Don't you realize that it is only himself who makes man a creature of any worth at all? Or woman either, since you will insist on separating them. We are not nice or kind or loving or anything unless we make ourselves so by giving and receiving those qualities all the time. Once the other things are allowed in, hate and unreason and fear and brutality, they spread, they're infectious. You don't know—you have never seen a person that has not received love and therefore cannot give it out again. You have probably never even seen an animal in that condition. Humans have to tame each other by endless love and patience in order not to be brutal.'

'I'd rather be a wild animal than a tame one. Lions and tigers are splendid, and noble. And at least natural.'

'There's nothing splendid or noble about the untamed jungle. Only the stench of blood. Like that woman. She was a perfectly nice and respectable woman and she had made herself *smell* of violence.'

'But you can't love and be patient against wickedness. It's cowardly.'

'You must. It's the only hope. You must love and love and love it until you have beaten it to its knees.'

'The suffragettes are beating Asquith and McKenna to their knees anyway without wasting time on loving them.'

'They aren't. They are only holding the whole thing up. They have only done harm, because only harm can be done by the means they use.'

'But splendid things have been done in a thousand different ways by the use of such means. And if you believe in a cause it is glorious to suffer for it, and die for it if necessary.'

But they had to stop, because there was someone standing quietly watching them. It was Edmund, who, finding himself with half an hour to spare, had walked to meet them. They did not know how long he might have been there.

'How could you?' Alice turned on him furiously. 'How could you stand there and listen like that?' And she turned and walked quickly back the way they had come. He ran after her and took her arm.

'Please come back. I had only been there a moment.'

'No, I am very angry.' She pulled away from him. 'How dare you stand there laughing at us? How dare you?'

'I am truly sorry. I was not laughing. You were quite right in what you were saying. Only I think perhaps you take too gloomy a view of human nature. But I was so interested, so—so excited that I did pause a moment, but only a moment. Please, Alice, please forgive me, I can't bear it if you won't.' She had changed from the demure and dutiful governess into a creature of passions and extravagances and of course he loved her the better for it.

She became calmer. They walked on to tea, and were in consequence of the little scene less formal than usual and more animated. After that day Edmund knew that his love for Alice was a serious business, but he was not yet sure what he was going to do about it.

It was about this time that Reggie Mather warned Aylmer about Horgan. Reggie Mather was a fat jovial banker, the descendant of a long line of fat jovial bankers of Swiss origin, and a back-bench Conservative M.P. of reliably right-wing views. Aylmer had told him that Philip was going into Horgan's firm of stockbrokers and had asked him whether he knew anything about it. He said that he didn't at the time, but a few days later he came up to Aylmer in the smoking-room and said, 'I made a few inquiries about your fellow Horgan, by the by. Didn't hear much to his credit, I'm afraid. I should try and get your nephew out of it as quick as you can, if I were you. It seems he's a real bad hat, this Horgan, been in trouble a couple of times before he struck lucky in South Africa. He's making a good deal of money now, apparently, mostly speculating on his own account, playing the markets. He started this stockbroking firm with a fellow called Miller who'd been in the business some time and had quarrelled with his own firm. It's doing all right for the time being, but it's not his only interest, and I shouldn't like to think what your Philip might be drawn into if he joins him, especially if he's new to the game. This is in complete confidence, mind you, but from all I hear Horgan's not to be trusted. Not the sort of chap we like to have in the City. I should get the boy out of it if you can.'

'Thanks, Reggie. I'll certainly try. I'm most awfully grateful to you.'

Perhaps Aylmer thought that Reggie was exaggerating, or perhaps he thought that Philip was sharp enough to cope with Horgan, or perhaps he thought that all stockbrokers were untrustworthy and that it was only to be expected, or perhaps he was merely over-optimistic and hoped it would all turn out all right in the end. Whatever the reason, all he did was to say to Philip next time he saw him, 'Oh, by the way, my inquiries about Horgan didn't elicit much in his favour. You want to be careful with him.'

'His reputation isn't the best thing about him, I'm afraid,' said Philip carelessly. 'I can handle him, though.'

'I must say he seemed all right to me,' said Aylmer

conciliatingly. 'Perfectly straightforward, I thought. Typical business man, of course, but the sort of person you know where you are with.'

'He's all right,' said Philip.

'I dare say you are quite right to go ahead,' said Aylmer. Perhaps it was just that he wanted to avoid a scene.

Chapter Eleven

Cynthia had been to Ascot.

She had come home early in order to rest before dinner, leaving Violet with her future parents-in-law, the Moretons. As she opened the door of the flat she heard laughter from the drawing-room. She went in and found Kitty, Alice and Philip. They had just finished tea. When they saw her they stopped laughing and stood up.

She refused the offer of tea and said she would go and take off her hat. A moment or two after she had shut the door she heard their laughter begin again. She sat at her dressing-table and slowly pulled out the long hatpins.

She thought, I am tired, I won't go back there, the children don't need me, I will lie on my bed.

But she sat on at the dressing-table, meeting her own gaze, but thinking nothing.

Soon there was a tap on the door. 'I am just going. May I come in and say good-bye?'

'Of course.' She stood up.

He came in.

'It's dark in here.'

'Don't turn on the light.'

'Why not?'

'I like it. It's soothing. I'm tired.'

'Did you enjoy yourself?'

'Of course. I always do.'

'Then why are you tired?'

'I don't know. It was hot.'

'Lie down.'

'I am going to.'

'Have you taken off your shoes?'

'Yes.' She sat on a chair and leant one arm on the back of it. 'Philip?'

'Yes.'

'You know I never interfere. But it is to some extent my responsibility. I mean, Miss Benedict.'

'Oh, Alice. Do you know, I rather like her.'

'I had noticed that.'

'She doesn't like me. She likes Edmund.'

'Edmund?'

'Yes, Edmund. The young heir.'

'But you don't mean—I mean, she cannot expect . . . ?'

'She doesn't expect anything. She is very docile. All the same I think she is quite attracted by me. She disapproves of me. She's rather a prig, you know. That's why Edmund appeals to her. But I think I have a certain sort of dangerous attraction for her. It's rather a challenge, I suppose. And how shocked poor old Edmund would be.'

'Please don't talk like that, I don't understand why you do it.'

'But I never shock you, do I? You only pretend. And I believe that secretly you would be rather pleased if I were to violate Miss Benedict.'

'Philip!'

'In some sort of strange way you would be gratified. It would satisfy that urge towards violence to which you will never admit.'

'You are talking complete rubbish.'

'After all, you want me to be a fine manly man, don't you, a credit to my sex? You know what happens to sons who never grow out of loving their mothers, don't you? And as you are always pointing out, you are my mother, more or less.'

'No. I don't know what happens to them.'

'They take to nameless vices and are absolutely no use at all to a good woman.'

'I think it would be a great pity if any son were ever to grow out of loving his mother, but she is bound to hope he will have no vices at all, even ones with names.'

'Mayn't he pick his nose? When no one is looking, I mean.'

'I'm tired and I can't understand you. Please don't make me wrestle with you in a struggle which I don't understand. I suppose you are joking. No, don't answer, then at least I can hope that you are. Go away now. Come and see me again tomorrow in a kinder frame of mind.'

'I didn't come to see you today. I came to see Alice.'

'Please go now.'

'Yes, Mother. Good night, Mother.' He moved towards where she sat. 'Don't glimmer at me so sadly in the darkness.' He bent to kiss her on the cheek.

She took his hand and looked up at him. 'How is it possible to understand so little someone one knows so well?'

'And loves so much.'

'And loves so much.'

'How indeed? I might look in tomorrow. But you are never here.'

'Come to lunch. The Birrells will be here.'

'No. I want to see you alone. I will find you though for myself. I will take you by surprise. Now you had better rest. It is nearly time to dress for the next harlequinade.'

When he had gone she lay down on her bed. She cried a little, but then she fell asleep.

Philip went on to see Horgan.

James Horgan was, as Reggie Mather had reported, an adventurer; but he was not picturesque. He was small and firmly plump, balding, fat-fingered and glossy. His nose was blunt and his eyes, his most attractive feature, round and bright. He wore silk shirts but bought ready-made suits. The trappings of wealth did not appeal to him. He had imagination, but it was all applied to the making and manipulation of money; the spending of it was of no particular interest to him. He merely travelled first-class, stayed at the Savoy, bought silk shirts, and had peaches sent to him from South Africa in the winter. He came from Bradford, but called himself South African. He never thought, walking briskly into the Savoy with a cigar and a camel-hair overcoat, If my mother could only see me now. Not that he had anything against his mother, but he had long ago dismissed her from his mind. He had dismissed a lot of people, and things, from his mind: it gave him his singleness of purpose. He had such a facility for figures as amounted almost to a mental deformity. They grew and multiplied inside his head until there was no room for anything else.

When Philip went into his office in Threadneedle Street he was talking on the telephone. It was a small ugly office consisting of three rooms, a central one where the clerks and typists sat and one each for Horgan and Miller. A secretary was sitting by Horgan's desk, waiting for him to finish dictating the letter which the telephone had interrupted. When he saw Philip he waved her away and indicated to Philip that he should take her place.

'Yes, yes, it's coming along very nicely,' he was saying impatiently. 'It's no use being in too much of a hurry. Yes, we are going to push it a bit faster now. I know, I know. We shall be clear of everything by then. O.K. I've got some big buying on hand for this morning, as it happens. Just let me get on with it, will you?' He put down the receiver, saying, 'You're no use in this business if you can't keep a cool head. Now then.' He was in his shirt-sleeves. 'Want something to do?'

Philip nodded.

'You can go down and do some buying for me. There's a firm called Cape Enterprises, South African mining firm, been going several years, never done much good, quite a big firm, quoted on the London Stock Exchange, they're going to boom, struck gold. Now if you've got anyone who might be interested we can get them some shares at a very favourable price, but it's got to be done quickly. Know anyone with money?'

'Everyone I know has money,' said Philip. (This was his manner with Horgan. It was not unsuccessful.)

'Well, don't tell everyone you know. What about your uncle? Want to let him in on a good thing?'

'I might.'

'I'd go into it yourself too if you can. There's hardly an element of risk in the thing at all. But the news will break soon and then it will be too late.'

'I'll talk to my uncle as soon as possible. Thanks.'

'I'll give you the information before you go. Now here's a buying list. Go down into the market and get some practice.'

Money, thought Philip in Leadenhall Street, lovely old money. He skipped briskly round an old gentleman in a top hat. Christ I'm going to be rich. Oh Edmund, my dear fellow, I thought you wouldn't mind if I dropped down for.

a day or two to show you my new Bentley, and this is Flossie, and Dossie, and, oh yes, Alice—you remember Alice?—quite a transformation, isn't it? An amusing little dress, Poiret ran it up with his own hands to my design. Indecent?—nonsense, my dear fellow, the latest thing, Empire style, you know. Careful with that luggage—that's Johnson, my man—got a little something for you, something to embellish the old home, don't you know. Picked it up in Paris last week—Titian, yes, quite amusing, don't you think? We've come straight from Ascot, little horse of mine won the Gold Cup—yes, wasn't it a bit of luck? How's the Bar? Briefs rolling in, I expect? Be buying Titians yourself next, ha ha.

'Ha ha,' he laughed aloud.

Poor bloody fools, I'll show them. Oh my dear old Asquith, what would I do with a peerage? No, no, all I care about is the good of the country. Well, if you absolutely insist—why not? Why not, indeed? And from Leadenhall Street out into Old Broad Street and the City workers going home and the hansoms. What a simple affair life is, an affair of knowing what one wants and of not being sidetracked by inessentials, abstractions, words you have heard but which mean nothing. Nothing, nothing, nothing. Not after Doctor Freud, anyway, not that any of them have ever heard of him, poor outdated meaningless—oh my Christ, why does she love me, what does she mean, love? She doesn't know what she's talking about. I'll show her, I'll . . . The river, the barges, the lamps, the warm dirty smell. Why are there so many people, why don't they get a move on? A feeble clerk and his anaemic girl. Damn them. Why am I alone? No one knows I am here. Why am I here? Who am I? Why am I excluded? Where are my people? Why doesn't being alone make me feel proud? Ah damn them, I'll go and find Cindy. I ought not to have left her like that without a word, I ought to have written. 'Cab? Flood Street, and quick,' Quick, before I am lost in the crowd.

They seemed to be waiting for him in a high dark room, portentous: Cindy and the painter whose studio it was and for whom she worked, the white-faced man with the red beard sprawled across an armchair in the opposite corner, the group of three solemn men who had been talking by the window, and the tall black-haired man in full dress uniform of the 14th Hussars at the time of the Duke of Wellington who was standing superbly alone in the middle of the room. But he was only the landlord who lived in a dream world. 'I'm going out to dinner,' he explained kindly. The painter was telling Cindy about his neuralgia: she looked in his mouth to find out if it might be caused by holes in his teeth. The three solemn men were talking about how to finance a literary review, and the bearded man was asleep.

When he had made his explanation the landlord relapsed into a splendid silence. He was a man of property, immensely handsome but deluded. He had a collection of military uniforms which had been left to him by his grandfather. He liked to put them on and wander about the house making quiet battle-cries in his deep mellifluous voice. He could tell you every detail of most of the major campaigns of British military history. He sometimes went about the streets of Chelsea in one or other of his uniforms, looking distantly down his fine long nose and humming *'Marlbrouque s'en va't en guerre'*. He was widely respected in the neighbourhood for his perfect manners and his habit of scattering largesse without discrimination in the shape of half-sovereign pieces. People said of him that he was happy, but his large dark eyes were awash with doubt.

When Cindy had finished looking into his mouth, the painter said, 'Hallo Philip,' without much enthusiasm.

Cindy said, 'Oh, it's you.'

The literary men went back to their argument.

'I was passing,' said Philip, discouraged.

'You can take us out to dinner if you like,' said Cindy.

He did. The three men went on talking about the review all through the evening. Towards the end they quarrelled rather badly. One of them went away, saying he could get a job on the *New Statesman* any time he liked, another said sensibly that he would go home in that case, and the third made a loud and impassioned speech about literary technique to which no one listened. By this time they were in an underground night-club in Soho run by an alarming old lady of outstandingly foreign appearance, who pounced on the painter and dragged him towards the door with furious energy; she pummelled him and abused him in some Scandinavian tongue until he left, then she explained that he had looked as if he were going to be sick. The martial landlord, who was still with them, his dinner engagement having turned out to be mythical, stood up and began an elaborately worded protest. She sat him down firmly but kindly and he began to recite poetry.

The red-bearded man, revivified, began to talk about a new heaven and a new earth. Other people joined in. Philip and Cindy went back to the two-roomed flat in Kensington he had taken when he left the Army. She kept him awake by coughing. He lay with his head full of waking nightmares in which an immense, superbly uniformed figure swayed and loomed and boomed, 'Half a league, half a league, half a league onward . . .'

Philip saw Aylmer. He had arranged to look in at the flat before dinner. Aylmer was already dressed for dinner when he arrived. Understanding that this was to be a business discussion, he led Philip into the tiny dark room which he used as a study when he was in London, and offered him a cigar. Philip refused, but accepted a Turkish cigarette.

He explained the advantages of Cape Enterprises.

Aylmer said, 'Of course, if it will help you in any way, I will certainly go to whatever figure you suggest. I think the best thing would be for you to have a word with Eldridge about it. He deals with all my financial affairs. Tell him I want to make an investment in this thing and arrange whatever you think best with him. Make it a sizeable investment, we might as well do the thing thoroughly. He's just sold those houses on Clapham Common that your Aunt Marion left me, so he might as well use that money. He'll drop me a line about it, I dare say, and I'll send an immediate answer telling him to go ahead.'

'Thank you very much,' said Philip. 'I'm sure old Horgan will be pleased at my bringing in new clients. Indeed I think that's the object of my existence in his eyes, that and a slightly mistaken idea he has of my respectability—but what I really hope is that it will make a good quick profit for you. That's why I told you about it.'

Aylmer rose from his chair, smiling. 'And why I'm going to do something about it is in the hope of helping you get off to a good start in your new enterprise. I'm more interested in that than in a quick profit.' He stubbed out a half-smoked cigar, and said, 'Shall we see if Cynthia is in the other room? I know she would like to see you before you go.'

When Philip told Horgan that Aylmer wanted £10,000 worth of shares in Cape Enterprises, Horgan said, 'If you drop a word to show who they're for when you're buying them it mightn't do any harm, let people know Horgan, Miller act for Cabinet Ministers these days, what?'

Philip did mention it, thinking he was merely pandering to Horgan's vanity. But, Horgan was not a vain man. He was concerned only to stimulate interest in the shares of Cape Enterprises.

Chapter Twelve

Cynthia was listing wedding presents in a pretty vellum-bound book adorned with tumbling cherubs and cornucopias overflowing with fruit. Violet had lost count and needed help so Cynthia listed while Violet at the desk tried to keep up with the thank-you letters.

'The Misses Bethell,' Cynthia wrote, 'garnet bracelet; Lucy Lady Hampden, four silver and tortoiseshell menu-holders; Mr. and Mrs. Brodrick, 8 vols Kipling's works; Colonel Stewart, silver and ivory paperknife.' 'Violet, Nancy Green is coming in to fit your chiffon blouses, had you forgotten?'

'Yes,' said Violet. 'Bother. I said I would go for a ride with Kitty. Never mind, if she comes punctually I might still have time.'

'Have you done the Tamworths?'

'I'm just finishing it. It's rather gushing, I'm afraid, but it was such a divine brooch that I can't help it. They are darlings, aren't they? Anyway Maud is terribly gushing herself, so it won't matter. There, I think I'll go up and get ready for Nancy. Then we needn't waste any time.'

'Yes, I should. Tell them to send her straight up.'

'All right. You don't want to see the blouses, do you? They're sure to be all right. And then I'll go for a—oh sorry, Granny, terribly sorry—I must rush.'

'I wish you wouldn't dash about so,' said Mrs. Weston coming into the room. 'It looks undignified and is a bad example to Kitty.' But Violet had gone.

'I wondered if I could help you at all,' said old Mrs. Weston to Cynthia, who rightly understood her to mean that she was bored and wanted to talk.

'I am worried about Moberley,' Mrs. Weston went on, not giving Cynthia time to take her up on her offer. 'He is being persecuted by Beatrice. She has him in some sort of thrall, and yet the moment she leaves him alone he hurries back to Ellen, who is much more suitable for him. I think you should have a word with Beatrice.'

'Good heavens, I couldn't possibly interfere in Beatrice's relations with her admirers,' said Cynthia, shocked.

'He's not an admirer, that's just the trouble. He's a helpless victim.'

'But what could I possibly say to her? She would be horrified. We never discuss that sort of thing.'

'I thought perhaps some sort of general warning,' said Mrs. Weston rather vaguely.

'She would be very surprised,' said Cynthia. 'It is not at all like me to make a general warning.'

Mrs. Weston smiled reluctantly and walked towards the open window.

'Is Aylmer coming this evening?' she said, looking out into the sunlit garden.

'I think so,' said Cynthia.

'He is overworking,' said his mother.

'I know, but the summer recess will be here before very long.'

'They may prolong the session.'

'Oh, it is surely not so bad as that. You mean, over this Irish business?'

'The European situation is not very good.'

'But it is never very good. Everyone seems to think it better than usual at the moment. I sat next to Mr. Lloyd George at dinner last week and he said that the external situation was the best it had been this century.'

'I don't think Mr. Lloyd George is much of an expert on foreign affairs.'

'He is very clever. You are always so gloomy. Are you thinking of this Serbian affair?'

'Not particularly. I am not thinking of anything particularly. Except Aylmer and his share in the Government.'

Cynthia wrote, 'Mr. and Mrs. Arbuthnot, Auction Bridge case.'

'People are too easily bullied by circumstances,' said Mrs. Weston.

'You mean that Aylmer should do more in some way or other?' said Cynthia

'I should like him to express what he stands for, to give words to it,' said Mrs. Weston, 'rather than just *be* it. His father, you know, was a much noisier man.'

'Perhaps he thinks some things are too deep for words,' said Cynthia. 'Or for the hurly-burly of politics.'

'He is over-fastidious,' said Mrs. Weston. 'And nothing is too deep for words.'

We had read in the papers about how the Archduke Franz Ferdinand and his morganatic wife, the Duchess of Hohenberg, had been shot on a visit to Sarajevo. We had been shocked, and had felt sorry for the Austrians, and had sympathized to some extent with Mr. Horatio Bottomley's 'John Bull' posters which said, 'To Hell with Serbia'. But I do not remember much talk about a general European war.

Aylmer came by train. He did not care for long journeys by car.

He sat in a corner seat in a first-class carriage, alternately reading the *New Statesman* and looking out of the window at the passing sunlit countryside.

The only other people in the carriage sat in the corner farthest away from him. They were a young couple, and he decided that they were extraordinarily attractive. They looked as if they could neither of them be more than twenty, though she was pregnant. He was a dark-haired, well-dressed young man with particularly soft large grey eyes; she was dark too and looked as if she might be wearing rouge. She had huge sad brown eyes—perhaps she was foreign?—her voice was so soft that he could not distinguish whether or not her accent was an English one. Their only luggage seemed to be a guitar case which was on the rack above them and a battered attaché case which

69

was beside them on the seat. During the course of the journey the young man opened the attaché case, disclosing some tattered sheets of manuscript and a packet of sandwiches. The sandwiches were large and inelegant, and looked good. They ate them with evident pleasure, not furtively as people often eat sandwiches on trains; their white young teeth closed on the meat shamelessly. The young man brushed away the crumbs from the girl's dress: they had fallen on to her stomach and he brushed gently because of the unborn child but without self-consciousness and without any extra tenderness because their whole attitude to each other was one of tender care.

Aylmer speculated about them, listening to their conversation as well as he could. They spoke quietly, but they seemed to be talking about how they were going to live—they were going to a cottage somewhere which he knew already but which she had never seen. He gathered from one or two things he heard that they were short of money. But they were travelling first-class: this seemed a piece of charming improvidence. Aylmer decided that he must be a young man of good family whose literary interests had taken him into Bohemia where he had found the lovely girl (the guitar was hers Aylmer decided), married her, and been cut off by his family. He was a Little Billee who had married his Trilby: it was delightful.

It occurred to Aylmer that he himself had an indirect influence on their lives. He was part of a government under whose ordinances their life would be lived, a government which in spite of all its conflicts, its undercurrents of interest, its occasional muddles, its failure, inherent in the mere fact of its humanity, to live all the time up to its best ideals, would not mislead them, would not interfere with their love, would see that such things as food and a decent education for their child and a roof over their heads would be available for them, in spite of their lack of wealth; and this, of course, they would hardly know or notice, thinking no doubt that politics was nothing to do with them, despising the politicians probably.

He began to go over again in his mind the complicated negotiations with two or three Conservatives in which he had been involved for the past few days, trying to find a formula for peace in Ireland. Now that, he thought, that would be a consolation, to have achieved that. And, as well as a consolation, a gratifying political advantage, So he sat thinking of the frontiers of Tyrone and Fermanagh, while the young people murmured in their corner like pigeons.

When he got out at his station he said good night to them in a friendly manner, and they rewarded him with two charmingly serious smiles.

He found Cynthia at her lists.

The wedding presents were being kept in the billiard-room, where they were to be displayed on the day before the wedding.

Cynthia was alone there, among the packing cases and the gleams of silver and mother-of-pearl, on the floor, reading from a leather-bound volume of George Meredith's poems, a present to Violet from her former governess, Miss Grainger.

She looked up when he came in, smiled but did not move.

Leaning over to see what she was reading, he quoted from memory, ' "Shy as the squirrel and wayward as the swallow"—ah, how appropriate—"When her mother tends her before the laughing mirror"—is this how you feel?—

' "Tying up her laces, looping up her hair,
Often she thinks, were this wild thing wedded,
More love should I have, and much less care.
When her mother tends her before the lighted mirror,
Loosening her laces, combing down her curls,
Often she thinks, were this wild thing wedded,
I should miss but one for many boys and girls." '

Cynthia arched back her neck and groaned. 'Horrible!' she said.

'Horrible? It's perfectly charming,' he said, surprised.

'It isn't, it's revolting, it makes me feel sick.'

He was shocked. 'You used to like George Meredith.'

'Well I don't any more. Silly old man.'

He was annoyed. He walked away. 'I didn't think I should find you in this sort of mood.'

'I'm not. I mean I'm not in any sort of mood, particularly. But really, Aylmer, it is so false, that, and futile.'

'I don't think it is false and futile in the least. It may

have, if you like, a touch of sentimentality about that particular verse. But then I always thought mothers did feel sentimental at the thought of their daughters marrying. Fathers certainly do.'

'Oh really, if you mean that because I don't like a poem of George Meredith's I haven't got the proper feelings about Violet's wedding—that's too ridiculous.'

'I didn't say anything about Violet's wedding. Though I suppose it must be that which has had such a bad effect on your temper.'

'There's nothing in the least wrong with my temper. I was in a particularly good temper, as a matter of fact, sitting here reading. I suppose it is because you have had a tiring day.'

'You suppose what is because I have had a tiring day? It's most certainly not I who am in a bad temper. I had a very pleasant journey down and was looking forward to a peaceful walk round the garden before dinner.'

'Then it must be the sight of me that has put you in a bad temper,' she said distantly, bending her head to sort out the books.

'I am not in a bad temper,' he said.

There was a long silence. He stared out of the window. She aimlessly sorted books.

'I didn't think I should find you like this,' he said eventually in a hurt tone of voice. 'It has been a long week. I hardly expected to find this sort of thing when I came home to snatch a few days' precious rest.'

'What sort of thing?' she asked flatly.

'You in this mood.'

'I have already said I am not in any sort of mood,' she said.

There was another silence.

'I wonder what you would do if you had to run the country,' he said musingly, 'if organizing a wedding reduces you to such a state.'

Silence.

'And then they want to give women the vote,' he said.

She still did not speak.

'I'm sorry, that wasn't fair,' he said, with an effort. 'I really am rather tired. Things are very difficult at the moment, you know. This Irish thing is getting more and more tricky and the Opposition never let up, and it's not as if everything's entirely smooth in the Cabinet itself, as you know. I really must be able to relax when I get home. It's enormously important to me. You know that.'

Her voice trembled. 'Of course. How could I fail to know it? Hasn't it always been important?'

He turned to look at her, surprised. 'But of course it has. Why not?'

She had covered her face with her hands. 'Why not? Why not indeed?' She murmured. Then, opening her hands, she threw back her head and looked at him. 'Why not why not why not?' she cried. 'It's what a home is for, isn't it, and a wife too? To provide comfort and relaxation and distraction from the real matter of life. To make a nursery world, to be both the nanny and the toy. And nannies don't need comforting themselves, do they, and a toy only needs a new dress if it's looking depressed . . .'

'I don't understand you,' he said blankly.

'Why can't I have any needs?' she went on. 'Why can't I need help or distraction or—oh, how you despise women!'

'That is perfectly untrue,' he said. 'I am a great admirer of women, generally speaking. It's true that I don't trust emotionalism.'

'Emotionalism,' she said scornfully. 'What does that mean? You mean emotions. Haven't you any emotions?'

'You of all people, know that I have. But I don't believe in giving in to them entirely. I believe in reason, and discipline.'

'But I don't want to be reasonable and disciplined all the time!' cried Cynthia. 'I want . . . I have other . . .' But she could not explain.

She put her head in her hands again, sitting still on the floor among the wedding presents; and after a time he went away, and walked round the garden alone.

There were the nightingales in the valley, and the air full of roses and dew, and the fox in the undergrowth, stealing the strawberries, striped by the moonlight with patterns of brambles: it was from all this that the house emerged, lit within, like a ship breasting the waves of moonlight, nightingales, movement and roses. Old Mrs. Weston paced the deck, backwards and forwards, backwards and forwards, the valley before her, the nightingales bubbling their song in the thorn-bushes by the thicket where the fox cubs waited for their mother's return; and in the different lighted rooms behind her only Ellen slept, the kitchen-maid, who went to bed early because she had to get up at 6.30 a.m.; but all the others were awake, and in action.

Kitty was in the bath, but her mind was active. She had entered into correspondence with Miss Sylvia Pankhurst, who had written to her, in answer to a letter of hers, to say that she did indeed need help in her work for the East End Federation of Working Women. She had gone on to suggest, tactfully, that it might be a good idea if Kitty, before doing anything dramatic like running away from home, came down to one of her meetings in the East End one day when she was in London and could escape for a few hours with a friend perhaps. The letter managed somehow to convey to the sensitive Kitty that Miss Pankhurst doubted whether she understood in the least what such work involved; not that Kitty minded that, for she felt herself perfectly capable of responding to the challenge and proving Miss Pankhurst wrong; but the problem was how to escape, and whether if she took Alice into her confidence she would risk Alice's taking an altogether opposite view and preventing her going at all.

When she had finished her bath she went along to Alice's room.

Alice, as usual in the evenings, was writing a letter home; or at least she had in front of her a large sheet of paper on which she had written, 'Dearest Mother and Father'; but after that she had only written Edmund's name in various different writings and sizes all over the paper.

Alice had often been in love. Ever since she could remember she had had a habit of falling for people, in such a way that her mind would be nearly always full of the then object of her affection, and though she would pursue her ordinary affairs without much loss of efficiency her mind would still be dwelling on the person, on his features, form, speech, on their last conversation, repeating literally hundreds of times words they had spoken, incidents which had passed between them, a touch of hands or a glance, imagining, again with endless repetition, a disclosure of mutual feelings, an embrace. Since this state of mind was so familiar to her, she was not in the least afraid of accidentally betraying her feelings, nor of their interfering in any way with her work as Kitty's governess;

she did not try to conceal their true nature from herself, but she felt capable of controlling them, nor did the prospect of their leading to unhappiness disturb her. She felt herself capable of dealing with unhappiness too. In spite of her dreams she could not seriously think that there was likely to be a happy outcome. She believed that Edmund liked her but thought that the difference in their social situations would prevent him from even considering marriage. She did not, of course, think of any relationship other than marriage: quite apart from any views of her own she would have thought it impossible for Edmund to entertain such an idea. She had been kissed on several occasions by the treacherous Irish curate—once or twice rather passionately—but that was the extent of her experience.

When Kitty came in she covered up the piece of paper on which she had been writing and said reprovingly, 'I thought you were in bed.'

'I've come to say good night,' said Kitty. She was holding Miss Pankhurst's letter. 'Alice, if you were me, what would you do?'

'About what?'

'Well, about life, and all that. I mean, I am condemned, aren't I, to a certain existence, to coming out next year, finding a suitable husband, living out the rest of my life running his house and supporting him and doing a few good works and organizing parties.'

'The great majority of women are condemned, as you put it, to something of the sort. I mean, to growing up and getting married and being a wife and mother. Is it such a terrible fate? If you mean that you don't like the way of life of the social class into which you have been born, I agree that at your age it is a little difficult to break away from it, but in a year or two you will be able to decide for yourself how you want to live, and you have quite a strong enough personality to be able to carry it through if you choose to be unconventional.'

'You mean I must wait? But I can't bear waiting. And besides, they might marry me off while I was still biding my time, and then I should never be free.'

'No one will make you marry if you don't want to. And if you have an adventurous disposition you will probably marry a similar sort of person and then you can both be adventurous together.'

'Alice, how dare you be so unbearably sensible? And you know perfectly well it is not as easy as that. You know there would be tremendous difficulties if I tried to do anything in the least unconventional, and I don't mean only from my own family. Anybody else, outside our sort of world, is bound to think that someone like me must be a complete fool. I want to do all sorts of things, and find out about everything, and make things happen, and end up as Prime Minister—you're not to laugh, I should be much better in politics than someone like Edmund, for instance—I mean, when I know more. Oh, I can't bear, I really can't bear, the thought of next year, and all the idiocies.' She sat down on Alice's bed and looked at her seriously. 'Do you know,' she said. 'I was thinking a minute ago, in the bath, of running away and going to live in the East End, and working for women's suffrage. But that would have been silly, wouldn't it?'

'Very,' said Alice.

'Because I am much too helpless. I have never even walked down a street by myself. And I should be no use. And worse than that, I should be using those people, and their serious cause, for my own ends. I should be using them for my own private rebellion. Every brick I threw at a window would be a brick thrown from the inside at the windows of the house I was born in. And that would be wrong, wouldn't it?'

'Yes,' said Alice.

'Well, Alice. I do wish that you would help me to educate myself, I mean seriously, not just to read the *Oxford Book of English Verse* and make tea-party conversation. And then in time I might be some use. I should like to be some use. Is that sentimental?'

'Not in the least,' said Alice. 'I think you are quite right. But I wish you would let me talk to your father about it. I really think you would find him extremely understanding, and he will have to help if you're to do things like going to lectures and so on next year when you are in London. Will you let me sound him out, very carefully, and see how it goes?'

'I suppose so,' said Kitty. 'I suppose he would understand. He always does. It is irritating in a sort of way, don't you find?'

'No, I don't think I do find it irritating.'

76

'Perhaps it is just that it makes me feel guilty. Do you think *he* is any use?'

'I most certainly do,' said Alice.

'But the Liberals,' said Kitty. 'I think when women get the vote they will all vote for the Labour Party.'

'Good heavens, why?'

'It has much the best intentions.'

'Liberal intentions are rather good too.'

'Things have changed. Granny, of course, is a Marxist.'

'She would be awfully bad at sharing everything with everyone else.'

'But she says there is no room for love in a capitalist society.'

'In theory, perhaps. But in practice there seems to be room enough.'

'Less and less, Granny says. I think she is really an anarchist, more or less. Or perhaps they are the same thing, I am not sure. Of course really she thinks things have gone to pieces terribly since the great days when Grandpapa was alive. I suppose it's in the family really. It's no wonder I've got it too. I think I'll be the first woman Prime Minister in a Labour Government. You can be—well, what?—you're so sensible—I think you'd better be Home Secretary. Shall we abolish hanging?'

On the way back to her own bedroom Kitty nearly ran into Beatrice, Cynthia's maid. Beatrice was walking along the passage, carrying a brass can of hot water, when Kitty came swirling round the corner in her dressing-gown and all but bumped into her. Beatrice drew back against the wall and gasped out 'My God! Can't you look where you're going!' before she could stop herself.

'Beatrice!' Kitty was amazed by her harsh tone. 'I'm sorry. I'm awfully sorry, Beatrice.'

Beatrice made an effort. She was trembling so much that the lid of the can rattled. 'I beg your pardon, Miss Kitty. It was the shock. It gave me such a shock. I spoke hastily.'

'It's all right. I am sorry. Are you all right?'

'Yes, I'm all right now. I'm sorry, Miss Kitty.'

'Good night, Beatrice.'

'Good night, Miss Kitty.'

Beatrice walked on, still breathing heavily. Her face was white. She was in a bad state of nerves. She was consumed by love for Ralph Moberley and by jealousy of Ellen, whom she rightly suspected him of preferring: she appeared to be literally being eaten up by these passions, as a candle is consumed by its flame. There is a theory that violent unhappiness or frustration can cause cancer: whatever may be the truth of that, something was killing Beatrice.

Hugging her seeds of destruction to herself with her hot-water can, she walked irregularly on and into Cynthia's bedroom, where she put down the can and covered it up.

Cynthia came in as she was leaving but was too preoccupied to do more than murmur a good night.

Cynthia and Aylmer very seldom quarrelled. When they did she did not know what to do about it: usually she waited for him to come and apologize to her; and usually he did; and then she forgave him.

This time it was a little different because she knew that she had been unreasonable; so when he did not come to her, she went into his dressing-room and said, 'May I come in?' rather hesitantly, standing in the doorway in her long silk dressing-gown with her hair down.

He was already in bed, sitting up, reading. He looked at her across the top of his knees, against which his Herodotus was leaning.

'Of course,' he said.

He looked very neat in bed, his hair brushed and his striped silk pyjamas buttoned up to his neck. He was wearing glasses, which he had lately taken to using for reading.

She came in and sat down on the end of his bed.

'I am afraid I was rather silly,' she said. When you have had a quarrel with your husband, a quarrel known to both of you to have been caused by nothing more than tiredness—a mutual lapse—you try to make it up before you go to sleep that night. This is a rule. Of course. But if your husband looks at you from such a distance through his new reading glasses and smiles politely as to a stranger or perhaps a constituent—what do you do then?

You still try to make it up.

'I'm sorry,' she said.

And if the kindness with which he is just about to forgive you fills you with a resentment so intense that you frighten yourself?

She bowed her head, looked at her clasped hands. 'I know I was being tiresome—and when you had just come back.'

'Please don't think about it any more,' he said from beyond his knees. 'Let's just forget it.'

'Yes,' she said.

His eyes had wandered back to his book.

She still sat there without moving, thinking, I will not show him that I know he is punishing me.

She put her hand on his knee.

'It's kind of you,' she said.

He put his hand on top of hers.

'You see,' he said. 'It's so important to me, you and all that I find here, all that it means to me. Believe me, politics is a wearing business sometimes—sometimes I don't know why one does it at all—and at the moment it's hard and nasty, and I long to be free of it and be with you. If you could be patient with me just a little longer, perhaps in the summer recess we'll go away together, just you and I by ourselves, before we go to Scotland. Violet will be married, Kitty will stay here with mother and Miss Benedict. We'll go anywhere you like, Wales or Brighton or anywhere, or Paris if you'd rather, or Nice. You shall choose. Can you be patient with me until then?'

But now she responded without an effort, ashamed. 'Of course! I know what it is for you, I know it, don't think I don't. We'll have a real rest together, it will be lovely.' She rested her chin on his knees, beside her own hand. 'I shall think about it. Don't worry about me.'

He stroked her cheek with his finger. 'Good night, my dear.'

'You want to read before you sleep. I'll go,' she said, staying.

'Yes. A page or two of my good old friend. There's nothing like it.'

'I suppose not.'

'Good night, my dear.'

'Good night.'

She glided away, turned at the door, but he was already reading. She watched him a moment, the thought in her mind being, We shall soon be dead; then she went back to her own room. He did not look up. When she had gone he closed his book, turned out his light, and lay down.

Chapter Thirteen

'I am not used to telephoning people at their offices.'

'You are not used to telephoning people.'

'No but—you are busy, I suppose? Working, calculating things? Juggling with huge sums of money?'

'I can spare a moment. I have a certain way of adjusting the telephone which leaves my hands free for juggling.'

'I see. You haven't been to see me, to see us. I suppose you have been too busy?'

'Do you want me to come and see you?'

'Of course.'

'And you telephoned me to say this?'

'Why do you sound so surprised? I am . . .'

'My mother after all. Quite.'

'I didn't telephone you only to ask you to come and see me, and if you are still in a tiresome mood I don't want you to come and see me. I want you to buy me some shares.'

'You? Gambling on the Stock Exchange?'

'You are buying some for Aylmer. I should like some too. I want to make a speculation, it would amuse me. I don't know anything about the Stock Exchange. Why can't I come and see it?'

'You wouldn't be allowed in. Besides, it's very dull.'

'Oh. Well, then, I see you don't want to share the experience of your new occupation with me so I will leave you to your juggling. You are at least coming to the wedding?'

'Of course. But it is not for some time.'

'Only two weeks.'

'I will come and take you for a walk in the park at half past five.'

'What an extraordinary time for a walk in the park.'

'Would you rather I took you to a *thé dansant* at Claridge's?'

'Of course not.'

'Then I'll see you at 5.30.'

'But I have to . . . Oh, very well. But you will buy me some shares?'

'How many?'

'How much do they cost?'

'If you mean the ones I told Aylmer about, they are

going up. They're now standing at 19s 3d.—they've gone up 3s. since last week—but they're still a good buy according to Horgan.'

'I don't know in what units one buys shares. I mean, ones or hundreds?'

'I would say hundreds.'

'What about 500 then? Would that be the sort of thing, do you think?'

'Anything you like. Make it less if you don't want to risk so much. I'll get you 100 if you like.'

'But Aylmer has bought thousands, hasn't he? And Edmund too I hear. I think one does it on a bigger scale than just 100. Make it 500. I think that would be suitable.'

'All right. I'll get you 500.'

'Thank you, Philip. Good-bye.'

'I'll see you at 5.30. In your hat.'

Philip, descending, a young apprentice in an old profession, one of a crowd of respectable young men wearing the blue buttons that proclaimed them beginners, felt himself a merchant going down into the market to negotiate, bargain, exercise the subtleties of the eternal merchant mind; and the gentlemen in top hats he saw as ancient traders, the jobbers lolling round their pillars, the money-changers in the temple. And I belong here he thought. In this den of thieves.

It had not in the least the appearance of a den of thieves: more perhaps that of a place in which a respectable old profession was practised, a profession sufficiently old and sufficiently respectable to have dispensed with outward shows, for in spite of the neatness of dress (most of the members of the Stock Exchange at that time still wore top hats), the surroundings were shabby, the floor dusty and covered with little fallen pieces of paper; the whole having the look rather of a crowded railway station, with untidy notices pinned up here and there giving the times of the trains. There were even one or two portly officials wearing a uniform not unlike that of a guard on a train—they were known as waiters, and Philip had yet to discover what, if anything, was their function. He meant to ask Smith some time.

Smith was Horgan, Miller's senior authorized clerk, the man who actually executed most of the firm's dealings.

Philip was not yet authorized to deal; being a 'Blue Button', all he could really do was to take messages to and from the office and the market, and observe. He had Horgan's assurance that as soon as his period of training was over he, Horgan, would see that he became a full member of the Stock Exchange with as little delay as might be. In the meantime he asked Smith as many questions as their mutual antipathy would allow.

Smith was both embittered and insecure. Philip seemed to confirm his worse suspicions about everything. Smith had good judgment: he had always had it and it had led to his downfall. He had worked for one of the best firms on the Stock Exchange, a firm which had done brilliantly both for itself and for its clients. Smith had shared in its success, had basked in the favour of his employers and of many of their clients, who had had a way of praising him, of saying, 'Ah, but we know we owe it all to Smith—he's better than any of you—he's unerring—he can nose out a good thing anywhere—never lets us make fools of ourselves when we think we've got a tip' and all the rest of it. With the result that poor Smith became over-confident, and began to make little sorties in his own account, and got himself seriously into debt. He was rescued by his employers but he had to leave them. Now he worked for what he knew to be an inferior firm, and, worse than that, they paid no attention to his advice, and, worst of all, everybody in the market knew of his history; or at least he thought they did, which was as bad.

And so he resented Philip. And Philip resented him, for his unwillingness to part with information, his obvious reluctance to accept without verification any messages from Horgan which came through Philip, and his general air of a bad old butler who knew more than he should and was only waiting for the right opportunity to use his knowledge.

Already Philip, who had powers of quick assimilation, felt sufficiently confident to tease Smith, to shock him by flouting a few of the many tiny rules and conventions which to Smith were inviolable. Throwing paper darts, as well as other forms of manly ragging, was in order, according to Smith, because it was traditional; but talking in too loud a voice about one's dealings, saying aloud things which should only be written down, failing to respect the older members—these were bad. Only that morning Philip had with pointless elaboration insisted on showing the way out to a fat old gentleman who had obviously been coming and going in the Stock Exchange for years; this had outraged Smith, though the fat old gentleman himself had taken it with apparent calm.

So that it amused Philip to go up to Smith, as he did now, and say quite loudly, handing him a piece of paper. 'The Cabinet wives seem to be after Cape Enterprises too now, as well as the entire Cabinet itself. And there's another big order from Godfrey Isaacs.'

Smith went perfectly white in the face and hissed like a snake through his teeth. Several faces turned and stared at Philip in blank amazement. Since the market was, as always, crowded, a great number of people had heard him. He turned and walked away unconcernedly, noticing as he went that there was a larger crowd than usual round the pillar where the jobbers who dealt with mines sat: Cape Enterprises was already moving quite rapidly; there were several figures in red after its name on the list above the jobbers' heads indicating rises in price since the start of that day's business.

Horgan sent for him and told him that he had been overdoing it, that Smith was threatening to resign, and that he had better keep quiet for a bit. 'Besides, we've got quite enough interest in the thing now. We don't want it all to go up in smoke.'

'Why do we want interest in it?' asked Philip.

'I'll tell you about it later on, don't worry,' said Horgan, exuding his usual air of confidence. 'Anyway we don't mind if the shares go up now, because we've got what we want for ourselves. But we'll play it quietly for a bit, shall we?'

'All right,' said Philip. 'When do you expect the news to break—about the gold, I mean?'

'Couple of weeks I should think,' said Horgan. 'Look here, do you want to know about this little company I've got here? I was just looking at all the papers when you came in. This is my own affair, nothing to do with Horgan, Miller. Property. Want to have a look? You can help me quite a bit with it if you want to. And look here, I shouldn't advise any more buying of Cape Enterprises at the moment, for yourself, or family or friends—don't want the thing to get out of control, do we? Now about this property deal . . .'

'I think I ought to go and apologize to Smith first, oughtn't I?'

'Yes. Do that. And then come back.'

Cynthia was putting on her hat. What a hat. Hats were like that that year, an exuberance of osprey feathers, tulle and all the rest of it; but this one was on such a scale as to make its frivolity rather grand.

And she herself? She gazed into the mirror, placing a hatpin. A woman of forty, or, rather, forty-two. Leaning closer, she saw wrinkles round her eyes, a few on her forehead. But she could have been years younger. I have had so few troubles, she thought.

A happy upbringing, life in the country, friends, a triumphant season, an early marriage to one of the most handsome and best-thought-of young men of her generation (they had been very young but had overruled their parents by their single-minded devotion, their confidence, even, in a way, their beauty). A son at nineteen, two pretty little girls thereafter, a life at the centre of the life of her country, of her time; admiration, interest, stimulation, a sense of purpose (she believed in Aylmer's work, and in a lesser way in the usefulness of her own contribution; she believed, not without humility, that she was part of an enlightened *élite* bringing peaceful reforms to the most civilized country in the world)—well, then, what more could she want? There had been a few bad moments of course, half-forgotten frights of childhood, small betrayals of the schoolroom, much felt at the time, and after marriage the usual adjustments to be made, his way or her way, his friends or her friends, how to deal with him when he was cross, or tired, or ill; but all this so cushioned round with comforts and consolations of all kinds as to be as painless as possible. There was the problem of Aylmer's mother, who interfered and had an unusual amount of intellectual arrogance, but then old Mrs. Weston was not altogether without tact, and Cynthia had grown fond of her and to appreciate her astringence. Then there was the time after Kitty was born when she had been ill. That was the worst time. After that she had felt she had in some way or other lost her innocence, because she had known too much about pain and, worse, despair; because everything on which she had been used to rely had seemed to fall away from her and she had felt hopelessly alone and the days had dragged bitterly and she had shouted at her nurse, and had wished to die. It had left her with a feeling of guilt, because she felt that it had been a test and that she had failed it; it had also left her with a faint unarticulated doubt at the back of her mind, a feeling she had never had before, so faint as to be hardly there, but a feeling that if that was what it was all to come to, if that was how it was to end, then the present moment must be made to release everything it had, to make it worth it. In other words, after her illness she was more selfish than she had been before it.

But her life had resumed its easy flow. So why should she have had this restlessness lately, or whatever it was?

It might be, she thought, something to do with being over forty; with being spoilt, and used to praise, and fearing that it might be growing less sincere; with facing the fact that it was time now for her to change from being a beauty into being a wonderful person, and realizing that it was a good deal harder to be a wonderful person than to be a beauty. Or it might be something to do with her children, that they were now grown up and did not need her; but then Kitty, she supposed, did need her; all the same, she somehow could not feel that even Kitty would not have been perfectly all right without her. It had been different when they were younger. Indeed with each of them she had felt, in spite of nannies, nursery-maids and all the rest of it, that she was quite extraordinarily linked with them, extraordinarily essential to them, in their first few years, as if in some odd way the birth process were not truly over until they were five or six. After that she was much more detached; she loved them, and admired them, and thought them beautiful and clever and self-sufficient; and it seemed to her only right and proper that their formative influences should now be coming from other people and not from her. She felt that even Kitty, in spite of all her extravagances of temperament, had a sort of basic equilibrium which meant she was not to be worried about; they had perhaps inherited it from Aylmer, this fundamental soundness.

For she had Aylmer.

But she had been to a concert at the Queen's Hall and had heard a Schuman piano concerto and had had to hold on to the arms of her seat to stop herself from jumping up and running away—running where?—she did not know—out into the street, her hair flying, holding up her skirts, running down Langham Place. It would have been absurd in someone of her age, pathetic merely. Philip had been sitting beside her.

Philip, with his odd position in her life, his detachment, his questions, his cruel jokes, his bright observant eyes, Philip was—well, what?—a great comfort surely?

Putting on her hat in front of the mirror, she thought in all innocence, Philip is a great comfort to me; and when he came and was shown in and she said, 'You see. I am in my hat,' she kissed him on the cheek and said, 'You are a great comfort to me,' taking his arm as though they were already walking in the park.

The bridge in St. James's Park, overlooking the lake bustling with ducks, and beyond the lake and the trees the clustered minarets of the Foreign Office; that was where they paused and Philip leant over the parapet and said, 'I thought you didn't need comfort.'

'Everybody needs comfort.'

'Against what?'

'Comfort is not against things.'

'For what then?'

'For—well, for being alive, merely.'

'What is wrong with being alive?'

'It's sad, isn't it? I mean, people die and that sort of thing—and one gets muddled, can't remember always what's the reason for things, and fails, and falls below one's standards.'

'You don't fall below yours, do you?'

'Of course.'

'Your high standards.' He looked at her profile; she was gazing at the greedy ducks. 'Where do you fall below them?'

He asked with kind interest, and without his usual mockery, so that she answered seriously, 'Sometimes I think I am not much of a help to Aylmer.'

He was disappointed. 'There I can't have an opinion.' He looked at the ducks too. 'How much of a help is he to you?'

'That's not the point,' she said, shocked. 'He is doing very important and exhausting work.'

'Why don't they have a war in Ireland? It would be rather fun. It wouldn't last long. We need a bit of blood-letting. We are getting fat and choleric, it would be like an application of leeches to the body politic. We should all feel much better after it.'

'You are not serious,' she said mildly.

'Of course I am serious. A brisk fight would clear the air.'

'It is wrong to kill people.'

'Of course. That's why it's so exciting.'

'You are ridiculous.'

'Not at all. We should all enjoy it. Think of Aylmer taking a shot at F. E. Smith. I think I should be on the other side, I should be an Orangeman. Edmund and I would be on opposite sides. We might kill each other. Think of that for tragic drama.'

'I don't want to think of it.'

'But you would enjoy it really. People like terrible things to happen to them. They thirst for drama and tragedy and to sup full of horrors.'

'I think you have a very odd view of human nature.'

'Not nearly as odd as yours. You believe in the perfectibility of man.'

'Yes. I suppose I do.'

'You think he is getting better and better, and that soon there will be no more wars and people will love their neighbours as themselves.'

'I can't say I see much hope of it in the immediate future. But you must admit it's desirable.'

'Not in the least. I think it would be a crashing bore.'

'Oh dear. Why do we always quarrel?'

'It is not exactly quarrelling.'

She laughed and turned to look at him. 'No. It's not, is it? Come on, let's walk. I shall have to go back soon. Edmund is coming round. He is going with Violet and a whole collection of people to some party on the river, and I want to see him. Aren't you going to it?'

She had taken his arm again.

'I haven't been asked,' he said. 'I am not such an eligible party as your son.'

'You do pretend to be cynical,' she said. 'Sometimes people marry for love.'

'Would you marry me if you were looking for a husband? Wouldn't you think you could do better?'

'You would tease me too much. That's why I wouldn't marry you.'

'If I didn't tease you. If I asked you very nicely.'

'Oh look. There's Edmund. He must have been to the house and come to look for us. He's going the wrong way. Run after him.'

'We can walk this way, then we shall meet him.'

'But—oh very well. How handsome he looked. You wouldn't shoot him, I'm sure, if you were an Orangeman.'

'But you love me better.' He closed his right hand suddenly over hers as it lay on his left arm. 'You do, don't you? You do, you do.'

'Philip—no, please—you gave me such a shock.' She was a little breathless. She tried to pull her hand away. 'Please, Philip.'

'But you love me better.'

'Oh really.' She began to laugh. 'You are absurd. I don't do anything of the kind. I love you all equally.'

He loosened his hold on her hand and stroked it gently. 'You don't really mind when I bully you, do you?'

'No.' She smiled at him, her gaze no longer disturbed.

Edmund was walking towards them.

He kissed his mother on the cheek. 'You're looking very well,' he said. 'How are you, Philip? They told me at the house that you were out here, so I came to find you. It's a lovely evening, isn't it? Have you been having a pleasant walk?'

Chapter Fourteen

Now it was high summer.

At Charleswood the lawns were turning brown, but the roses clothed the walls and draped the trees with undiminished vigour, the white ones lustrous in the shade. Kitty and Alice in the schoolroom with the blinds drawn talked languidly through the hot afternoon and pursued their private dreams: old Mrs. Weston opened the windows of the Silver Wraith and tied an amber motoring veil round her head, hardly interrupting the harsh flow of her voice into the speaking tube: Moberley nodded, his mind on his engine and regardless of his girls.

In London the parks were even more burnt up; but the air was cooler by the Serpentine than in the stifling streets. In Bond Street where Wilfred and Violet were slowly walking, the pavements were less crowded than usual; it was too hot for shopping. He had said he would buy her a diamond watch as well as the brooch he had already given her as his wedding present; and so they walked up Bond Street, but very slowly because of the heat, and soon they would stop and go somewhere for tea even if they had not found the watch. They could always buy a watch tomorrow and in the meantime walked slowly, she in a shady hat and muslin and he in his bowler, pleased with themselves.

Cynthia lay on her bed in Queen Anne's Gate, her curtains drawn but not excluding the sound of traffic, of a passing horse, feet on the pavement and the distant boom of the clocks of Westminster. She was so relaxed that she seemed to float, borne on clouds of warm air, she being pale and fragrant, and vigorous too, like the roses, for as long as she could rest in the afternoons she did not mind the heat. In her mind there was nothing; a floating greyness, faintly violet, nothing more. There are people who spend years of mental and physical discipline in trying to achieve this state; to Cynthia it came naturally when she was, as she would have put it, in the right mood. She had been in the right mood less and less often lately, but the gift had not yet deserted her. It was probably the reason why sleeplessness was an affliction entirely unknown to her.

It was not unknown to Aylmer who had been sleeping badly for the past week. He was in the House of Commons, playing chess with the Home Secretary, and intermittently discussing an irritating Cabinet meeting which had taken place that morning; and then just as the game was settling his mind, and just as they seemed to have agreed on the necessity for a private meeting with the Prime Minister to urge on him the need for brisker action over certain labour problems, McKenna had to start talking about the Balkans, and Europe, and German ambitions, endlessly tiresome points which he did not want to think about on such a hot afternoon. He tried to dismiss it all with praise of the Foreign Secretary, but failed, and then McKenna used the phrase 'if it came to a showdown' and he was forced to contemplate the possibility of European war, which was a possibility he had been doing his best to avoid contemplating for the past two weeks.

'There's no earthly need for us to be drawn in,' he said. 'We have most expressly not committed ourselves, to France, or to Russia, least of all to Serbia. Our only real commitment is our guarantee of Belgian neutrality, and anybody who flouts that is mad—bringing the whole world into conflict like that—no one can afford it. Can't we get a European conference of some sort?'

But it was no good; the situation remained worrying, however he expostulated. He could not help being aware of how little he knew, beyond the broadest outlines of policy, about how his country's foreign affairs were being conducted.

After his game of chess he sent a note to John Morley asking if he could come and see him. Those members of the Cabinet who most cared about preserving peace must get together: there were several on whom he felt he could not rely to put that consideration high enough on their list of priorities.

He sat for much of the afternoon in the library working out arguments and how they could most cogently be put to Grey and Asquith; later a note came from Morley asking him to dine that evening. He decided to go back to Queen Anne's Gate in order to have a little time with Cynthia.

When he got there he found that she was out. They did not know when she would be back, but expected it would not be long because they knew that Mr. Philip was expected later.

He asked for tea and thought, waiting for it, Why always Mr. Philip, and never Mr. Edmund?

Edmund and Alice had started a correspondence. It was quite a step. Those were the days of letter-writing, but, still, she was the governess. He had started it, on the pretext of continuing a discussion they had begun about G.E.

Moore, and now they wrote regularly, keeping their correspondence a secret known only to each other.

Alice had a pretty, flowing hand. She enjoyed the actual movement of writing, the feel of her pen on the paper, the formation of the letters: that was partly why she wrote so much; letters home, diaries, now copiously to Edmund. She wrote about Kitty: 'I have been talking to your father about her. We were very serious, alone together in the library, discussing her future—it made me feel very old and responsible. To my surprise he was quite angry at the thought of her wanting to do something a little different, even if she doesn't go into politics, which is what she says she wants to do at the moment. I had not realized quite how much of an anti-feminist he is. I knew, of course, that he had spoken against the granting of female suffrage, but I thought that was because he disapproved of the methods the women's organizations have been using, but it is something more than that. I suppose you probably share his views. I don't think we have ever discussed it? Of course the sad thing is that I share them too in a way, but after all how can anyone expect us suddenly to find our way unaided about a man's world, after centuries of oppression and lack of education? But poor Kitty—anyway he was chiefly, I think, insulted that she should not be entirely satisfied with all that he provides for her in the way of charming surroundings, stimulating conversation and all the rest of it. Even the most enlightened parents are so easy to offend, aren't they? And then he said that the only proper object of a woman's life was marriage, and having children, and creating, jointly with her husband, a home—not, he said, merely ordering the meals and seeing that the silver is cleaned, but making a positive atmosphere, the most creative thing most people can do—a moral statement, he called it; and that what is most important for Kitty is the finding of someone with whom to share all this, and she will not do so if she goes exploring in foreign fields. And just as I was feeling completely defeated by this he suddenly capitulated and said that she may attend a course of lectures at the London School of Economics next summer if I go with her. So it seems that willy-nilly I am to be educated too. And you see he only said that out of a desire to do what was right and good. I do find it impossible not to admire your father. I know you do too, but

Philip is strange in his attitude to him, isn't he?—although I believe he really loves him as much as any of you do. But I think he suspects him of making assumptions which he ought not to make—I don't believe he does, I think Philip is wrong. I suppose it is some sort of envy on his part—almost everything is, isn't it?—I mean almost everything that seems out of order or that one can't at first understand, in oneself or others, seems usually to turn out to be some form of envy. But you are lucky to have such wonderful parents. Mine, though I love them dearly, are terribly dull—I wouldn't usually admit it, but they are, and my father disapproves of everything, really everything—life itself, and inanimate objects, and death—so what is left? I think in spite of their professional relationship he really rather disapproves of God. I don't do you? But then, probably in reaction against my father, I have gone to the opposite extreme, and approve of almost everything.'

'It can't last,' Mrs. Weston said, meaning the weather.

'Thundery,' said Moberley, inclining his head slightly so that his ear was closer to the speaking tube.

'I had the most extraordinarily vivid dream when I was resting after lunch,' said Mrs. Weston. 'I can't remember the details. Only the atmosphere.'

She could remember the details, as a matter of fact, but they were not suitable for Moberley. She had seemed to see Cynthia, in one of those flashes of apparently enhanced reality which dreams sometimes bring, floating through the air on a cloud, or bed, naked, immense, asleep, the still figure seeming, perhaps because of this mental trick which so clarified its definition, to be a matter of the utmost urgency. She could not imagine why a sleeping Cynthia should float thus demandingly into her consciousness.

'Meaningless symbols drop like pebbles into an empty mind,' she mused to Moberley, 'and are mercifully lost. Do you believe in dreams. I mean in messages, prophecies?'

He did, or course, though he thought a lot of nonsense was talked about that sort of thing.

The subject filled the rest of the afternoon more or less satisfactorily until she could say, 'Would you drive home now? I think it must be tea-time,' wondering at the same time whether in her increasingly cranky old age she might at last be becoming jealous of her beautiful daughter-in-law.

Cynthia returned to find Aylmer already gone.

'I wish I had known he was coming back. I could easily have been here. I was only wasting my time, shopping.'

Philip had been waiting for her.

'Don't look so worried,' he said. 'You'll see him in an hour or so.'

'No, he will be late. I shall be asleep. I sleep so much. Oh dear. Don't go into politics. You have so little private life.'

'I shan't. I should never be able to fool myself that my motives were honourable. But I thought playing political hostesses was fun?'

'It is, I suppose. But I have done it a long time. Besides, Aylmer is not ambitious enough for it to be really amusing for me. You have to be deep in intrigue for it to be fun for long.'

'Don't you intrigue?'

'No. Though I tell people how clever Aylmer is when they ask. Where are you going?'

'Back to my flat to bathe and change. I have to go out to dinner.'

'Where?'

'You are losing your pride. You don't usually ask.'

'I am only trying to take a polite interest.'

'I am having dinner with a girl called Cindy.'

'Who is she?'

'Worse and worse.'

'I am naturally interested in your friends. Particularly the female ones. I want you to marry and settle down.'

'You wouldn't want me to marry and settle down with Cindy. She is rather common and probably consumptive.'

She turned on him quickly and put both hands on his arm. 'You will catch it.'

'What makes you think so?'

'Philip, you must—I insist that you see a doctor. You may have got it already. I beg you, Philip.'

'Of course I haven't got consumption. I don't suppose she has either. I was exaggerating. She has a slight cough.'

'All the time?'

'All the time.'

'Please don't go on seeing her. Please get another one.'

'Another what?'

'Mistress.'

'How broad-minded of you.'

'Philip, seriously . . .'

He put his hand on her cheek. 'I should never find one as beautiful as Cindy.'

'Is she very beautiful?'

'Very,' he said, holding her face in his hand.

She looked into his eyes, 'Philip, if you love her . . .'

'I don't,' he said, his lips on her cheek.

She turned away, slowly. Then she said, quite coldly. 'You are surely old enough to stop pretending to be Byron or somebody.'

He did not answer. She walked across to the other side of the room, fiddled with a newspaper.

'Who are you pretending to be?' he asked.

'I am tired of your sort of conversation,' she answered distantly.

He sighed. 'Well, I must go. I sold your shares in Cape Enterprises by the way.'

'Sold them? But we'd only just bought them.'

'You made a small profit on the deal. But they have started to go down now.'

'Why?'

He spoke in a brisk, matter-of-fact voice, being embarrassed. 'I discovered, while running through his papers one day when he was out, what I think may be a possible connection between Horgan himself and Cape Enterprises. And I suspect, because such is my nasty nature, that he spread the rumour about the firm's discovering gold in order to boost the shares so that he can unload his own shares before the whole thing crashes.'

'I never heard of anything so immoral. You can't mean to say that that's the sort of thing that goes on on the Stock Exchange?'

'Not at all. Horgan is something of an exception.'

'Have you sold Aylmer's shares, and Edmund's?'

'Not yet.'

'But they may lose a lot of money. Surely you should sell them?'

'I should, yes,' Philip admitted. 'The truth is, Horgan won't allow me to. He has told Smith not to accept any more selling orders in Cape Enterprises from me.'

'He's admitted it then, admitted his part in it?'

'We didn't discuss it. He issued this command and told me that he would let me know as soon as I could dispose of those shares in which I was interested. He said he would see that my family lost as little as possible, if anything. I think it will be all right. He used Aylmer's name among others to promote activity in the shares. It's not in his interest to let him suffer. As soon as he's unloaded his own—and I suspect he's been doing so quietly for some time—he'll let me sell Aylmer's and Edmund's. They may lose a little, but it won't be anything to worry about.'

'Of course it will be something to worry about. They are not rich, you know.'

'I'll make it up to Aylmer as soon as I can if he does lose. Horgan is letting me in on a property company he's starting. That's to be a sort of reward for not making too many difficulties about this little business. And if there's anything in that, which there should be, I'll be able to make it up to Aylmer and Edmund. It's going to be rather awkward with one or two other people—I rather spread the thing around, I'm afraid. Still, it's my own fault. I ought to have seen what he was up to before.'

'Don't you bear any resentment?'

'Oh, I don't know. He made a mistake a long time ago in getting involved in the thing and now he's only trying to get out of it without losing his investment. Of course it's reprehensible, but what is one to do about it? It's all being done as quietly and discreetly as possible—he has not let the shares get too high—I think he will get away with it. And because I have helped him, though unwittingly, I shall be at an advantage.'

'What about your own shares?'

'I sold them with yours.'

'I can't understand why you couldn't sell Aylmer's and Edmund's at the same time.'

'I was going to, only he stopped me, as I told you.'

'It makes me feel like your accomplice.'

He said nothing, and she went on, 'Why shouldn't I tell Aylmer to sell his shares, immediately, through another stockbroker?'

'You could,' said Philip. 'But Horgan would know it was my doing.'

'What does that matter? Aylmer would have sold his shares.'

'And I would have lost my job.'

'Would you?'

'Yes, I'm sure of it.'

'Why do you want to go on working for someone like that?'

'I have no other way in there, as far as I know. And he is clever. On the sharp side of course, but he has ideas, he makes things happen. And he needs someone like me. This thing means more to me than the amount of money Aylmer might lose means to Aylmer.'

'Does it? Why?'

'Because it's my life. If Horgan takes me up in the way in which I think he might take me up, I stand to make a lot of money. Otherwise, I don't.'

'Is money all that matters then?'

'It matters a great deal. It does to everyone. Some people are more honest than others about admitting how much it matters to them, that's all.'

'I suppose it is because you have never had very much, have felt you had less than Edmund. But you have never really had to worry about money, have you?'

'I had less than anybody else in the smart regiment into which you put me.'

'You asked to be put there.'

'I know. That was unfair. I don't complain—how could I?—of the way I have been brought up. For heaven's sake don't take what I say as being *that*. But I want things, all sorts of things, and they can all be bought with money. Horgan could mean a lot for me. I'm not going to give him up because of this, leaving the possibilities unexplored.'

'So you will not sell Aylmer's shares until Horgan tells you you may. And Aylmer may lose a lot of money. But you will keep your job and your opportunity, which is not yet proven, of making the money you tell me can't really matter for Aylmer. It sounds a little . . . suspect.'

He turned away from the window and sat down on the sofa, leaning back against the cushions and looking across to where she stood on the other side of the fireplace.

'If it worries you,' he said, 'tell Aylmer to sell his shares.

It doesn't really matter to me all that much. Nothing really matters to me all that much.'

His figure, lax now against the cushions, his eyes yellowish like a lion's, not very large, rimmed with dark lashes, familiar, looking now without apparent subterfuge into hers, the white thin face, not happy but not, it seemed for once, concealing anything from her, he was so much more there and opposite her than anyone else could ever be: she could either remember from when she had been standing close to him, or still smell, the smell of his skin, as known to her as his yellow eyes.

'I don't know whether you are changing me in some way,' she said. 'A little time ago I would have told Aylmer to sell his shares.'

'Tell him now,' he suggested mildly.

She still looked at him.

'I suppose ordinary questions of morality hardly enter into these money affairs?' she asked humbly.

'I suppose they hardly do,' he said. 'It is all so unreal, you see.'

She moved round to sit in an armchair opposite him.

'I shan't say anything. I shall leave it all to you. But I wish you hadn't told me. As I said, I don't like the feeling of complicity.'

'I'm sorry. Try to forget it. It's not of great importance.'

They sat opposite each other without speaking, absorbed in a feeling of sadness.

Chapter Fifteen

Aylmer and Edmund walked beside the river, going home after visiting a tenant farmer down the valley. The flies were low over the water. Two or three blackbirds were singing in separate trees.

'The river is full of fish this year,' said Edmund.

'I wish I could spend more time here,' said Aylmer. 'As it is, I shall have to go back to London as soon as the wedding's over. There's this conference at Buckingham Palace coming up and I want to do a lot of preparatory work on it.'

'I'm glad you're in on that. Do you think you'll make them see sense?'

'I don't know. I find myself less and less willing to predict how other people will react to things. The more one understands the more complicated people's motives appear. But I think something ought to come of it. Have you heard any more of the Tewkesbury affair?'

'I think there is a reasonable chance that I could have the seat when Thompson retires, which he says will definitely be in not more than five years' time. It would fit in very nicely for me as long as I've got through my Bar Finals all right. Then I can have a few years' slogging at the Bar before I take on anything much politically.'

'Of course you've got through them. It sounds an excellent plan. I can't tell you how much I look forward to having you in the House. Whether or not we shall still be in power by that time remains to be seen—not that I myself wouldn't welcome a spell of Opposition, for purely selfish reasons.'

'It will be fine to have you to show me my way about. Oh look, a kingfisher, did you see?'

'I missed it. Where?'

They waited on the bank for the kingfisher.

Edmund had meant to say something, however tentatively, about Alice, but, knowing his father to be overworked, he felt unable to break into his present contentment, and so he said nothing for the time being.

The wedding was on 7th July—a Tuesday—and for several days before that the house was full of bridesmaids and relations. The Moretons were staying, a dull but well-intentioned pair—she was a knowledgeable gardener. Wilfred himself was staying near by with his best man, one of the Geralds. The other people in the house were mainly bridesmaids. Violet had decided to have twelve. Ida was among them, glowing in her golden way with vicarious happiness, and Margaret, and Cicely, and all the rest of them.

Violet herself was rather fussed. It had been a fairly short engagement and she had to have everything ready to leave for India almost as soon as they got back from their honeymoon.

Cynthia was calm. She had all the preparations for the

wedding perfectly under control, and since she had an exceedingly efficient staff she had nothing particularly exacting to do herself. She had enough energy to have undertaken a great deal more, had it been required. In the heat everyone else was easily tired, wanted only to sit in the shade; but she, though she did sit in the shade, could have done anything. Her white beauty, which might have seemed something to be shaded, with affinities rather with the moon, on the contrary thrived and gleamed in the hot sun.

On the Sunday evening before the wedding Philip, who was staying there for the week-end, took her for a walk and told her that he was afraid Aylmer and Edmund might lose more than he had originally feared over the Cape Enterprises affair.

'I'm counting on being able to sell their shares pretty soon. But Horgan told me last week that he didn't think I should be able to do it until the end of next week. And they're going down all the time, though no one seems quite to have caught on to what's happening yet. I'm going back to London tomorrow and I shall try my best, but if I don't succeed perhaps you ought to warn Aylmer and get him to sell them through someone else.'

'Has he never asked you about them?'

'No. It's not the sort of thing that interests him. Or Edmund either.'

'Do sell them as soon as you can.'

'You don't think you ought to tell him?'

'No. Not now.'

He had known she would say that. But he had not known she would say it so decisively.

'I am sorry to have made you my accomplice.'

'I am not sorry,' she said. 'But next time, let us be accomplices in something better.'

He stopped, sat on a low stone wall—they were walking down towards the wood—and said, 'I think you may be right, I think I am changing you.'

But she had forgotten what she had said a few days before. 'What do you mean, changing?'

'Are you coming over to my side?'

'As opposed to who else's side?'

'Aylmer's.'

She did not seem shocked, though she said, 'I don't

99

know what you are talking about. Don't be mysterious. Come on, I want to walk a long way this evening.' She held out her hand.

'I love you,' he said.

But she had taken his hand and pulled him to his feet.

'I know, I know, I love you too. Come on, I want to walk miles and miles. With no metaphysical conversations on the way. Just nature study, and a few appropriate platitudes.'

It was at the end of that day that Ellen the kitchenmaid slipped down the stairs in her bare feet, carrying her shoes, climbed out of the kitchen window, the bolts of the door being too noisy, and found Ralph Moberley waiting for her in the stable yard. He had been talking about how warm the nights were and how he had been for a walk late and seen badgers playing, and she had said, 'That's a thing I'd like to see,' and he had said, 'You should go one night.'

'I think I'd be frightened,' she had said.

'I'll take you. I'll show you where I saw them, the next fine night.'

'Mrs. Mount would never let me.'

'Come out quietly. She'll never know.'

So she crept out to join him, and they went across the stable yard, she rather giggly and excited, he rather moved by the sight of her bare feet, and all would have been well had not Beatrice, sleepless with one of her headaches, looked out and seen them go, and stored up the venom the sight released in her until it became too much for her to contain, and she spilt it.

Chapter Sixteen

Of course it was a perfect wedding. The sun shone, Violet looked sweet, we were all there and in our best.

The reception was in the garden. 'A perfect day,' people said. 'You couldn't have hoped for a better. It all looks so beautiful. A dream wedding.'

There is a photograph of all the bridesmaids walking

across the lawn in a long straggling line, out of step. They are wearing heavy white satin dresses, tight about the ankles, so that it is not easy for them to walk. Cicely is holding the skirt up with one hand so that a good deal of bony ankle shows above the black satin buckled shoe. In the other hand she carries, as they all do, an immense bunch of long-stemmed lilies. No, Kitty is not carrying lilies: because she had to hold Violet's train, of course. Kitty wears a shorter dress, but the same lace fichu round her shoulders and bosom, only hers ends in an artificial flower at the waist, theirs in high beaded waistbands. They are all wearing lace caps bound with a black velvet ribbon and bow, and upon the bow, perched like a feather, is a little bunch of orange blossom. Round their necks they wear a thin black velvet ribbon and a gold chain bearing an enamelled locket given to them by the bridegroom. Kitty's hair is about her shoulders: the others of course have theirs pinned up. They all wear long white gloves. Kitty's feet look larger than any of the others'.

Then there is the guard of honour, from Wilfred's regiment. There is a photograph of them with their helmets on so that you can only see the ends of their noses and their upper lips (the lower ones being concealed by the chinstraps), and one with their helmets off. Then they have put them on again and are lined up behind the bridesmaids and the bridal pair for the complete group. In Violet's album she has written all their names in her neat small hand and later has added in brackets what became of them in the war, so that we read, 'Tpr. Townsend (wounded 1914), Farrier French, Tpr. Moynihan (killed 1915), Cpl. Potter, Farrier Newbolt (reported killed 1918),' and so on. Cpl. Harper is very handsome. He apparently got through unscathed; but Cpl.-Major Thorp, who is nearly as good-looking is 'killed 1914'. As a matter of fact they are all rather handsome.

There are so many people in the larger group that Violet has only had room to write their initials. Under her own image she has written 'V.M.M.', the last letter heavily underlined. They are in the garden, posing in front of a yew hedge.

Cynthia had her own way of dressing. She wore very few trimmings in that year of the beaded fringe, relying rather on line and her own superb carriage. But her hats were enormous.

Here she is in the softest of grey chiffon, the skirt falling in fluted columns from the high waist, a high neck and long full sleeves, her hat a marvellous sweeping brim beneath a curling feather. She had quite a feeling for the dramatic: it was a good hat in which to look desolated by the loss of a daughter. But in this photograph she is not looking desolated (she did cry a little in the church): she is looking untroubled, talking to Lord Tamworth, who is exquisitely dressed himself from top hat to grey spats. He is leaning forward, smiling through his golden beard, telling her probably how beautiful she looks.

'How beautiful you look.'

'And so do you.'

'Impossible to believe the mother of the bride could be a creature so radiantly young.'

'Not when the bride herself looks sixteen. Do you think she will be all right, Tammy? Were we foolish to let her marry so young? She is only twenty.'

'Of course she'll be all right. The Moretons are a very nice family, and she's got plenty of common sense, your Violet. That's what's needed in a marriage, common sense, a decent upbringing behind you, and good manners. Don't you agree?'

'I suppose so.'

'Now there's a pretty pair, Ida and your Edmund. Are you doing any match-making there?'

'I hadn't really thought. It would be nice, of course. She is so sweet. Oh Philip, there you are. How was it, do you think?'

Lord Tamworth said, 'I see old Claygate, must have a word with him,' and smiled and bowed and walked away.

'Tammy doesn't like me. He thinks I am insolent.'

'So you are.'

'Only to you.'

'That is not true. But if it were true, why should you only be insolent to me?'

'Give me your hand.'

She gave it to him. He held it, twisting it slightly, and dug his nails into it hard, and then let it go. She withdrew her hand slowly, because people might be looking at them.

'I don't really understand you, Philip.'

102

It was true. She did not really understand him.

Edmund thought, What is the matter between Mother and Philip. Why are they looking at each other like that? Now he is walking off and leaving her alone, rudely, but there's Lord Moreton coming up to talk to her. Poor Mother, she has seemed rather nervy lately. But I suppose it must be a year or more since she lost that evenness of temperament I used to love most about her. Alice has it, that is partly why I love Alice. I wonder what is the matter with Mother. I suppose after all she is a little spoilt, though people always say she's not. Of course he has always given her everything she could possibly want. It's funny, people say how wonderful it must be to have a mother like that, such a wonderful person besides being so beautiful, and of course one is proud of her and all that, but it's him we really love. Now Philip is talking to Alice. I wish he wouldn't. I'll go over there, taking Ida with me. I don't like the way he looks at her. Have you seen the roses, Ida? How silly of me, you've been staying here all week! But we are walking towards them, that's right.

Philip, turning away from Cynthia, thought, I want her. And moving across the lawn as if in search of someone, I want her. Why have I fooled myself? Perhaps I have known for a long time. I don't know. I can't remember. I know it now, though. To rip off that hat and pull down her hair so that it's all round her shoulders and how long have I wanted to plunge my face into those breasts and feel the soft skin between the hip-bones: this is bad and won't do, it really won't, I'll have to do something. Alice in a governessy hat. Why is she so suitable all the time, silly little thing? Shall I . . . Why don't I come to your room tonight, little governess? After all I'm almost a son of the house, it should be an honour.

'Shall I come to your room tonight, Alice?'

She looked at him coolly. 'Why?'

'In the old-fashioned phrase, to lie with you.'

She had meant to embarrass him by her question and make him change the subject, but of course it had been a mistake, and she was unable to prevent a furious blush.

'Of course not. Please go away. I have to look for Kitty.'

But here came Edmund, protective.

Philip turned to Ida. He admired her. He thought, I wouldn't mind marrying Ida one day.

There is a splendid photograph of old Mrs. Weston. She is entirely in black, leaning on an ebony cane, talking to the Prime Minister. She wears a hat, top-heavy with black gauze, at one side of which reposes a large bunch of fierce black flowers: her dress is black silk and has a huge diamond pendant gleaming on the front of it. She wears several rings on her gloved fingers.

She was treated with respect by the Liberal leadership because of her late husband's worthy place in the annals of the party, but most people, including Mr. Asquith, were rather frightened of her.

'Are you going to let this Irish affair drift into civil war? Many people want it, you know.'

'I think you exaggerate there. Not many people surely? And I'm certain it won't come to that. People like to talk, you know, and make a noise.'

'It's dreadfully humiliating to be dependent to such an extent on the Irish vote. Don't you sometimes think of resigning and waiting until you can come back with a reasonable majority of your own?'

'No, because I believe that if you have been elected you have to govern as best you can in the circumstances as they are. And I still think that we can do it better than the other side.'

'But a civil war would be a terrible failure.'

'I don't believe we shall have a civil war. There are not quite enough foolish people about, although I agree with you that there are very nearly enough. There's this conference. I'm moderately hopeful of the outcome of that, and I think Aylmer is too, isn't he? I'm awfully glad he's in on that, it's so much the sort of thing he's good at. Did he tell you that it was the Monarch himself who asked for him?'

'No, he didn't tell me.'

'How typical of him.' He went on to tell her about it, and her criticisms were effectively stilled until other people came up to join them and the Prime Minister was able to slip away and talk to Ida, whom he found a much more agreeable companion. She prettily asked his advice about her reading and he gave it, gently patting her hand from time to time and exuding amiability.

Here is Alice, pale beneath her sober bonnet.

'Wouldn't you like a chair, Mrs. Weston?'

'Thank you, my dear, but I shall make my way slowly to that bench over there, collecting as I go one or two people to come and talk to me while I sit on it. Yes, an arm would be very kind. Standing is so tiring. But you're looking pale yourself. You must be tired. I believe you have done more work than anybody for this wedding.'

'Oh no, I have hardly done anything. Lady Weston has been wonderful.'

Lady Weston is always wonderful, you poor little thing, there is no need to sound so sad about it. Has she been bullying you, the wonderful Lady Weston? Here's something which might comfort you: you are the only underling I have ever seen Cynthia bully. So that is a distinction, isn't it? I wonder why. It can't be because you're too pretty. She likes pretty people round her—or she always has until now. Perhaps she is weakening, afraid of getting old, losing her power. If so, she's mistaken. She looks as beautiful as ever, a little more spiritual merely as the bloom of youth retreats but still *effleurissant*.

'She is *effleurissant* today, isn't she?'

'Oh yes.'

'Perhaps it's the thought of your own wedding which is making you sad?'

'Oh no.' Is it the blush that has brought tears into her eyes, or are they tears of sorrow? 'I'm sure I shall never . . .'

'There, there, I always cry at weddings too. Shall I tell you whose wedding I have been thinking of? Moberley's. He has decided to marry Ellen after all. I put it down entirely to my influence. But it is a secret, so you must not tell anyone. He is terrified of what Beatrice will do when she finds out. He is threatening to leave and run away with Ellen to escape her wrath. I am very worried about it. I have offered to talk to her myself, but he won't allow it. But it would be a disaster for me if he were to go. After all this wedding business is over I am going to try and persuade Lady Weston to give Beatrice her notice. It would be much the best solution. Especially as I think she is going mad. Oh Tammy, yes, you may come and talk to me over here. Edmund, take Miss Benedict to find some tea, she is quite worn out.'

They walk towards the table, not too close together.

'Are you really tired out?'

'No, it's nothing.'

'You look pale. Something has worried you. Is it Philip? Something he said? You mustn't pay any attention to Philip. He is always trying to shock people.'

'I know.'

'If you have any trouble with him, just let me know, and I'll come and knock him down.'

'Knock him down?'

'Don't laugh. I have often had to knock Philip down. And that's not boasting because he's very easy to knock down. Poor old Philip. He's all right really. Just a bit complicated.'

'I know.'

'I wish I could talk to you properly. I can see there is something. I've got to go back to London this evening, that's the trouble. I must be there tomorrow, and as Father's got to go this evening, I said I'd go with him. Will you write to me?'

'Yes.'

'No, but I mean tonight, before you go to sleep. Will you promise? And tell me what you have felt today—everything—please. And I will write to you too and tell you everything. You know, I have a lot to tell you, Alice. Oh dear, here's that old bore Claygate. Promise to write, promise.'

'I will, I promise.'

'I promise too. Look, here's some tea. Ah, Mr. Claygate, yes, it is pretty, isn't it? The garden is at its best at this time of year.'

My dear Edmund, Alice wrote in her imagination, I have decided that it would be best really for me to go back to Ireland. You see, I have let myself become too involved with all your family, and that is a mistake, and just the sort of silly thing I always do, and so I think I ought to go, because I've realized today more than ever before that we are impossibly different, that you belong to something extraordinary, a sort of sect, nothing to do with me, and that of course you will have to marry within the sect, and that—of course I know we have never said anything about marriage—oh dear—My dear Edmund, I am writing to tell you that I am going back to Ireland. By the time you get this letter I shall have left . . .

I shall be sitting in the garden reading and I shall look up and he will say . . . No, no, he doesn't know where I live. Besides, I shall get another job at once.

My dear Edmund, I have decided to get a job with a family that travels a great deal. First of all we are going to Australia . . . I feel so hurt. Where is my open mind? The Governess's Benevolent Society. First of all we are going to Australia . . .

If I could be alone a little, and could walk by the sea, I could turn all this into a gentle melancholy, a peaceful sadness. I could manage it then.

> 'Parthenophil is lost and I would see him
> For he is like to something I remember
> A great while since, a long long time ago.'

I hope my hair is not going to fall out like it did after Mr. Waters.

'Extraordinarily pleasant,' Aylmer was saying. He was standing beside Cynthia in the sun, looking round at the groups of people on the lawn. 'Extraordinarily pleasant.' He meant the garden and the weather, the agreeability of their friends and the beauty of the house, background to another soft explosion of family happiness, endeavour, love, decorum and achievement. 'I feel very proud of them all, don't you?'

'Of course,' she answered.

'I'm so sorry I have to leave tonight. You won't feel lonely with everyone gone?'

She shook her head, smiling.

'I'd have stayed if I possibly could, but I've this meeting at 9 o'clock in the morning and I must be there. It's all so important now. I'm afraid Mother's been bullying the P.M. again. I wish she wouldn't.'

'I think he is imperturbable.'

'Yes, but it is rather rude. Nice of old Curzon to come,

wasn't it? I thought he might not, he's been so hostile to all of us lately, politically. I think it's because of you that he came.'

'He's a dear.' But she was not really paying attention. She was looking for someone in the crowd.

'Although I regret going this evening I can't help thinking in a rather sentimental sort of way that anything I can do, well, it is helping to preserve all this, isn't it? And it's so well worth preserving.'

She smiled, affectionately.

'No, but it is,' he said. 'Everything that's best in English life has come from this sort of background, places like Charleswood. I've always been glad that we're so well rooted in this particular soil. It's the right one. I'd hate to have been born any higher.'

'You would have made a dear duke.'

'But you wouldn't like that.'

'Not in the least. Ah, there's Philip.'

'Were you looking for him?'

'I was wondering where he was. I wanted him to look after young Miss Moreton. She has been looking a bit left out.'

'Poor thing, she's very plain, isn't she? Is Philip coming up with Edmund and me?'

'No, he is staying until tomorrow.'

'Good, then you will have someone to amuse you. Otherwise I was almost thinking of staying and starting very early in the morning.'

'Oh no, please don't do that, I shall be quite all right. I am very happy about this wedding, you see. I shan't feel sad after it.'

'I'm glad. Nor shall I. Shall I suggest it to Philip, about Miss Moreton?'

'Would you? I'm just going to see if the tenants are getting all they want to eat and drink. Tell him I said he must, however much he may not want to.'

Oh no, please don't do that, I shall be quite all right, I shall have Philip. I have been looking forward to it all afternoon, to sitting with Philip after dinner and talking about the wedding and listening to him being unkind about everybody who was here. They will all have gone. Probably Mama will be tired and will have something on a tray in her room: I hadn't thought of that. And Kitty and Alice will be in the schoolroom. So we shall be alone. What a luxury. I shall have a bath and change into my green tea-gown, and we shall sit opposite each other. Really I would rather be with Philip than with anyone else in the world. I wonder if he will manage to get out of talking to Miss Moreton, wretched boy.

Because there was to be no party after the wedding, as had at first been planned. They had had the party a few days before, because Violet did not want to miss it herself and because this was to be such a busy week for Aylmer. And then the Moretons had thoughtfully said that they would go on to spend a few days with their friend who lived so near, the Gerald with whom Wilfred had been staying. And the bridesmaids were to be variously withdrawn into the bosoms of their families, and the guests, even the oldest of the aunts, some of whom seemed to have been staying in the house for weeks and weeks, were to disperse.

They will all go, Philip thought. I shall be lost.

'Cynthia says you are to talk to Miss Moreton. She says I am not to allow you to escape it.'

'I have talked to her.'

'You have? Oh. I wonder if Cynthia knew that. Or do you think she meant that you were to talk to her again?'

'I expect she meant that I was to talk to her again,' said Philip without moving.

Aylmer laughed. 'Poor Miss H. A very successful affair, don't you think?'

'Very.'

'Does it make you at all nostalgic for your Army days, all this military splendour about us?'

'Not in the least. They have faces like wooden soldiers. As an Englishman I feel very proud of them.'

'So do I,' said Aylmer, pretending not to notice Philip's tone. 'How's it going in the City? What about those shares you bought for me? Have I made my fortune yet?'

'No, not exactly. As a matter of fact, I am rather worried about them. I don't know that they were such a good investment after all.'

'That's bad news. Ah well, I suppose if you must have guinea-pigs they had better be your own family. But don't lose me too much. This is an expensive year for me, what with weddings and all the rest of it.'

'I know. I wish—but the thing is—well, I may have been rather misled. I'll try to put it right of course.'

Aylmer looked worried. He hated talking about money. He also, like most people, hated losing it.

'I expect you'll be able to look after it,' he said hopefully. 'After all you are in the know, where you are.'

'I hope so.'

'Look here, don't look so worried. I'm sure it will be all right. I can stand a little temporary set-back, I suppose. It couldn't amount to much, could it?'

'Well . . . I hope not.'

'I'm sure it couldn't. I mean, your chap said it was a good bet, didn't he? I won't even inquire if you like. I needn't know for a bit, you see. Eldridge will see to anything that has to be done. I needn't know for a bit, by which time I expect it will have been made good. I mean, they go up and down these speculative shares, don't they?

'Yes. Yes, I suppose they do.'

'That's what I'll do then. I'll leave it in your hands entirely, and not ask to know anything about in until it's all over. Oh dear, Mother's going round from one Cabinet Minister to another, telling them how to run the country. It is too naughty of her. I had better try and head her off. Get poor Miss M. some strawberries or something, won't you, like a good fellow?'

Strawberries for Miss Moreton. Lord, what am I going to do about those shares? If I sell them next week and put what money there is into something else . . . ? Surely Horgan can think of some means of recouping a little, after all he owes me something. Thank God at least I'm on the board of that property company. I'm learning to handle him now too. Why does Aylmer have to be so bloody nice about it? Aylmer. Aylmer. Aylmer. He didn't mind. He simply didn't mind the idea of losing £9,000. He didn't turn a hair. I bet he never sleeps with her. Imagine him naked. Well, he would be just the same of course. Nothing can change him. He is always the same. And yet in a sort of way he retreats from me, I can't feel his limits. Why didn't he make a fuss about the money? Why won't he talk to me?

Mrs. Weston was not bullying the Foreign Secretary. She was talking to him about birds, and his distant suffering face of a larger bird was bent down towards hers to hear above the surrounding talk the story of the redstarts that had nested in the garden that year, for the first time as far as she knew. But he had been on his way to find Cynthia to say good-bye, for he had only come briefly out of friendliness for Aylmer and wanted to leave, so when his host approached he began to make his excuses and they went off together to find Cynthia. Mrs. Weston wandered off through the crowd, frightening people with her stare and thinking, He feels as I do. I wish they would all go now, idle selfish creatures, so that the ordinary rhythm of the garden could reassert itself; he knows nothing can compare with one's love and knowledge of a place, as I love and know this place. I have been in love, but it never compared, for feeling, with some of my walks through the wood in May: people would be shocked if they knew that. It's something that's hard to share: one can share the pleasure of the recurrent events of the garden or the wood but not exactly that sort of ecstasy: it is sight, sound, smell, touch and imagination all exercised at once, the extraordinary sadness and at the same time rightness of the transience, the recurrence, the indifference to man's concerns. Well, I shall die in the spring, after a winter that has been hard to get through, when my resistance has been lowered; a spring cold will catch me and I shall die with all that great push and pulse outside my window, the smell of it coming into me, the shadows of birds dashing past to carry food to their young flashing across the sunlight on my bedroom floor. When you are my age you think about death nearly all the time. The love, you see, was too hard and demanding, and for much of the time one was too involved to know what was really happening. I did it well, though. It is a pity the nightingales have stopped singing now; we shall not hear them again until next year.

'We shan't hear the nightingales again until next year.'

'Yes, but you know,' said Kitty, to whom she had spoken, 'that hardly worries me at all.'

'You have got terribly untidy.'

'Bother.' She patted her lace cap hopefully. 'Is that better?'

'Hardly.'

'I like this wedding, don't you? I think everybody is being nice, even horrors like the Tammies.'

'You mustn't speak like that about old family friends.'

'They couldn't have heard. Do you think it would matter if I took my shoes off?'

'Yes.'

'They are terribly uncomfortable.'

'Never mind. Come and sit with me on this bench for a little and we will be unkind about people's clothes.'

Strawberries popping into Miss Moreton's little mouth, between her big irregular teeth, one after the other, fat red strawberries dipped in sugar.

'You're sure you don't want cream?'

'I like them better like this. They taste quite different with cream.'

'Or is it that you're banting?'

A blush. 'Oh well, I . . . But I do really like them without cream.'

Philip thought of Cynthia. The best thing in a way would be just the luxury of the first kiss, the softness of the mouth, its sad corners, the eyes closed, the lovely beginnings of laxity. Of course it wouldn't be like that, she would be horrified; but, then, she is so strange, so unsuspecting, one might have reached her mouth before she drew away. But it couldn't be more than a touch, I can see her look of outrage, she would . . .

'Yes, we have certainly been lucky with the weather.'

But I could make her, it would be better like that, I would hold her down, my fingers would bite into her soft upper arms, I would crush her, crush myself against her . . .

'But all brides look the same, don't you think? They all look radiant.'

Because obscurely she must want it. I couldn't want it so much myself otherwise. It must be so, she must want it. Do you want it, do you want my face pressed into your warm neck, my hand on your breast? Do you? For she was there now, she had walked up to them, smiling. He thought impatiently, Don't smile that stupidly understanding smile which means, Thank you for talking to the dull Miss Moreton. Smile the other smile, the smile of complicity, like you did the evening I sat on the wall, when I had told you about the money.

'Miss Moreton tells me she likes strawberries better without cream. Can't I get you some?'

My dear Edmund, it was in church that I realized it. I am sure you have no idea of this, but as a matter of fact you all behave in a slightly unusual way in church, I have always admired it before, even if it has sometimes amused me, but today I realized for the first time how horribly exclusive it is.

You walk into the church as if it were the house of some relation of yours with whom you were on friendly and familiar terms, and before the service begins you talk quite loudly, sitting in your family pew, looking about you: when you come in you kneel for a moment but with only that touch of deference due, as I said, to an older relation. The service is conducted in the way in which the vicar knows you like it, the psalms sung to the tunes you know, with no tiresome innovations, and the hymns, well, one or other of you has probably chosen them anyway, while consulting with the vicar about the lesson, which one or other of you will read. You like the hymns. You rise to your feet briskly and rather noisily when they begin, and sing lustily. Your father sings reasonably well, and the women's voices don't particularly stand out, but your hymn-singing is noticeably loud, cheerful and inaccurate. No one else sings much at all, except one of your cowmen whose voice is nearly as loud as yours and a little more in tune. You turn round sometimes to look at him when you are singing and you smile at each other and afterwards say, 'What would they do without us?'

You must remember that I have spent a lot of time in church one way and another, because of Father being a dean, and the differences between your sort of church and mine, though small, seem to me significant. Of course I know that you are patrons of the living and so choose the vicar, and I know that you gave the altar cloths and the rugs and most of the money for restoring the tower, and that the females of the family in Victorian times embroidered the kneelers, and that the monuments are mostly to vanished Westons; but during the sermon you either sleep obviously or make comments. I know that none of you snore, and the comments don't usually go much beyond a hearty 'Quite so, quite so' from Sir Aylmer, or a croaking 'Nonsense' from old Mrs. Weston, but—well, I wonder if you can see at all what I mean. Even today when the Bishop was there you were the same. Of course you were most respectful and charming to the Bishop, but a little as if he were your elderly relation's most trusted, most faithful, most loved by you all since you were children, upper servant. Anyway in church today all this struck me most forcibly and I thought for the first time that it was not a joke, that you were quite right. God *is* one of you and I am not.

Poor Miss Moreton. She faded away, and we did not notice her go. I wonder why Philip is staring at me. Is he wishing that they would all go and that it was already this evening? But it is Violet's wedding, my pretty daughter's wedding. I can't be wishing it were over. It must be that I am imagining that that is what he is thinking. I expect I am wrong anyway. Probably my hat is crooked.

'Is my hat crooked?'

'No.'

'I thought perhaps—you seemed to be staring at me.'

'I expect I was. I was wondering what you were thinking.'

'I was wondering the same about you. I expect, if we guessed, we would both be wrong, don't you think so?'

My dear Alice, was it we who had tired you, without meaning to? I know we can be demanding sometimes, and you are so good, you see, you do too much. Mother, for instance, is used to having everything done for her by someone else, she takes it for granted. I love you for doing too much, and for being too simple ever to think of not doing yourself whatever needs to be done. In fact I love you. I have got so used to saying that to you in my imagination that I could write it to you without any embarrassment or reserve. But you must understand, you do understand I am sure, that I can't do anything that would distress them too much, I must break it to them gently, let them get over Violet's wedding and then introduce them to the idea of you as their daughter-in-law. Because

Mother can be quite difficult sometimes. Not that that worries me particularly, we can cope with Mother, you and I. But Father—I know you understand, won't think it means I love you the less. I want it all to go quite slowly for us, I want the whole of the rest of our lives to be filled with it, with our development, I want it to be an eternal game of tennis, to and fro, to and fro, and we getting better all the time with practice, and never scoring, an endless sunlit game of tennis with the score for ever love all. You do understand? You don't think I ought to be in some way more dashing in my love for you? Because of course I will try to do whatever you want. Only you see the sort of person that I am.

Cynthia turned to Philip with her loveliest smile and said, 'I mustn't stand here talking to you. I can save you up for tonight, when we shall be alone.'

It made him dizzy for a moment, and by the time he had recovered she had walked away.

Edmund thought, I wonder why Philip is looking like that. I hope he hasn't been drinking too much. I know he said something to Alice which upset her. I wish he wouldn't do that. It's all right for me, I know old Philip, I don't take him seriously. I respect him, of course, for being different, for having some odd opinions. In his position I should be the same. I wonder what he really does think, though. We haven't talked properly for a long time. We used to, but he has been so much more withdrawn lately. It may be because he has taken a bit of a risk in leaving the Army and all that, and will be on the defensive with us until it has proved a success. He doesn't seem to talk to any of us intimately now, except Mother of course.

'Edmund, I am rather tired, I am going to go in. But I can't see Violet anywhere. I must see her before I go. Do you suppose she has gone to change already?'

'Sit down, Granny, and I'll go and find out for you. Oh Kitty, has Violet gone to change?'

'No, not yet, she's over there.'

'Granny's going in, she wants to say good-bye to her.'

'I'll go and tell her. No, you stay there, Granny. She'll come to you.'

'Kitty is enjoying herself.'

'Yes.' They are all enjoying themselves. So was I, until a

115

moment ago. Exhaustion comes on me so quickly these days; and then everything changes, it is like a dark cloud across the sun, the same scene but differently lit; oh no, it is not the same at all.

They all looked so pretty, a moment ago. Well, they look pretty now. But different.

She was sitting, waiting for Kitty to bring Violet to her, on a bench on the terrace in front of the house, looking down on to the lawn. At the end of the lawn was the yew hedge and beyond that, hidden, a rose garden, before the park with its fine clumps of trees. On one side of the lawn was the formal garden in front of the orangery; on the other a walnut-tree, longer grass, shrubs and trees with roses climbing them, that retreated into the distance, half wild and beautiful. Here where she sat the garden was tamed, the gravel paths carefully raked.

It is like a lake, the lawn. We sit down and watch the people skating, in a Dutch painting, in muffs. I wish Violet would come, there is a little cold wind. One could almost believe they were on the ice. If I half-shut my eyes because they are aching, the people more than ever seem to glide. The women especially. It is because of their hobble skirts; they had had to learn to walk like that. There is Cynthia, a superb skater, with attendant admirers a little behind, and Enid Tamworth, rather jerky, chattering all the time, in brilliant scarlet, startling among the surrounding sweet-pea colours of this summer. They do make a pretty scene, even when one has clouded them over with one's own tiredness and turned the smooth green lawn to ice: they are so pretty and smart and lively. I must not go to sleep. It seemed to be getting dark, it must be late. But no, of course it doesn't get dark until much later than this, this is the summer. I must open my eyes properly. But I can't, the reflections from the ice dazzle them. It is so bright. How can the skaters bear it, turning and gliding there, chattering and laughing? Doesn't it make their eyes ache? Groups form and reform, now a figure dashes across the ice to take another by the hand, to lead it away, gliding more slowly, hand in hand. How bright it is, and how active they are. If I shut my eyes a little more the dazzle goes from the ice; now it is only soft grey and transparent, so smooth, and under it shapes moving slowly, so much more slowly than the skaters on top. Fish, I suppose. But how can they breathe without air? Someone should make a hole in the ice; oh, but it is all right, there is a crack in it, I can see it quite clearly, it's odd that I didn't notice it before. So the fish will be able to breathe. Is that why they are so close to the ice, bumping against it from underneath, so as to reach the air? They seem very large fish. Such great round heads. But the crack! Is it safe for the skaters? Do they know? Shouldn't someone warn them? And with those great fish underneath. If they are fish. Why doesn't someone do something?

'Why doesn't someone do something?'

'Mother, good heavens, what's the matter?' Aylmer bent down towards her. Edmund was on the other side.

'You ought to warn them,' she said. 'You must do it, Aylmer. It's for you to do. You must warn them to get off.' She waved her hand towards the lawn.

'Do you mean to get off the grass? But I am reconciled to having it ruined.' He sat down beside her on the bench and patted her arm soothingly. 'It's all beyond my control. But it will be all right, don't worry.'

And here was Violet coming across the lawn towards her, her hand on Wilfred's arm, with Kitty beside them chattering; and the sun was shining.

'You have been a beautiful bride,' said old Mrs. Weston. 'Everything that we had all hoped and expected of you. Hasn't she, Wilfred?'

'I should say so.' Wilfred's eyes—face, indeed—glowed with pride, happiness and general enthusiasm.

'I do hope it hasn't tired you, Granny. Shall I look in to say good-bye when I've changed, before we go?'

'That would be sweet of you.'

'I will then. It will be quite soon, because we must go, mustn't we, Wilfred? I don't want to at all. It's been such fun.'

'I'll take you up,' said Aylmer.

Mrs. Weston took his arm, and they went into the house.

'It's been a wonderful day, hasn't it?' he said.

She agreed.

'You sounded worried just now,' he went on. 'Or had you been dreaming?'

'I had been dreaming,' she said. 'But sometimes I wonder if the life we lead is, in a sense, *real* life. I mean, do we not live as if we had already made the world fit for people to live in as we do, when in fact we have not done that?'

'But I think we have, as far as England is concerned.'

'Perhaps you are right.'

'I'm sure I am.'

'I don't know.'

'And aren't we all still working at it? You are always so general, you know, in your comments. To be particular, what more could I, for instance, do?'

'You do so much. I don't know. I only know . . . It is all to do with the requirements of love, which are endless. The demands are limitless. It all depends on your idea of yourself, and on Man's idea of Man. That's all that matters. There isn't any reality.'

'You are too metaphysical for me.'

'Kitty, now. You know, I think it is an excellent idea for her to do this course next year. She might be a teacher, or at least an influence. You see if humanity could be re-educated, re-directed . . . That must be where the hope is, in the education of the young.'

'Dear Kitty, she has some way to go herself before she starts directing others. Now here we are. Shall I ring for Fletcher?'

'I suppose you will have to. Unbearable woman. I shall have to listen to her inane comments on the wedding.'

'Never mind, think what a nice day you can have tomorrow, driving about going over the whole thing with Moberley. Violet is coming to say good-bye to you, isn't she?'

'Yes. I shall be all right now. Dear Aylmer. I wish everyone were like you.'

'It would be a dull world if they were,' he replied with his customary cheerfulness.

Philip thought, I really want to destroy them. They are so artificial, everything that they say means something else; everything is within the bounds of propriety, even impropriety. I want them to be blown away, the little bright bubble of their world to burst. Why? Because they irritate me, isn't that enough? I want them to be blown to all the corners of the earth, and all their little trinkets lost. I want them to be frightened of me, instead of saying, 'How nice for a young man to want to be a rebel,' I want them to learn what they themselves are really like, I want them to face it, I want them to own up. Why won't Cynthia be what she really is, why does she pretend to be this false creation of Aylmer's? I could create her, I am creating her now, but I would create her as she really is. And all the time the whole thing borders on farce. Why doesn't Cynthia clap her hands and say, 'Ladies and gentlemen, I should like you all to go home, I should like you to leave me alone with my nephew in order that we may make love'? Well, she doesn't say that because she doesn't mean it. Or if she does mean it she doesn't know she means it. Why doesn't she mean it? And can one be said to want a thing if one doesn't know one wants it? Yes, of course one can. And she must want it, she must. I must make her want it.

'You are rather naughty, Tammy. You are so gallant that soon nobody will believe a word you say about anything.'

He protested, expostulated, explained. Cynthia, not listening, thought, He is rather an old bore. I have always been fond of him, and enjoyed talking to him, and flirting with him, but today he strikes me as rather an old bore. I wonder if he has changed, or I, or neither of us? I would rather talk to Philip, flirt with Philip. Perhaps I am too fond of Philip. It is silly, I mustn't let it show. But he makes everyone else seem dull. He doesn't ever really let me know what he thinks of me. Of course he is fond of me, he must be, but I think he despises me a bit, he makes me feel foolish sometimes, and inadequate. It is funny, hardly anybody else makes me feel like that. But he must be fond of me. He talks to me, he comes to see me, even if it's only to torment me, he touches me, he said he used to be in love with me when he was a child. Perhaps he is more fond of me than he would like to be, perhaps he would like to despise me more than he does, I quite like that idea. But he has women, that mistress with the cough, he probably doesn't think of me at all, except as part of the background, his pseudo-mother. I know that's not true. I'm glad it's not true. But I mustn't be silly about Philip.

'Violet, darling, I think you ought to go and change.'

'I'm just going, Mummy. Where's Kitty? I promised she could come and help me.'

'I'll come up in a minute, shall I? You have so many helpers.'

'Yes, come and see if I'll do before I come down. Oh, there you are, Kitty. We're going up.'

Kitty went with her, and so did all the other brides-maids, to help her change into her going-away dress.

Philip thought as they passed him, Ida would be a good marriage for me; she is rich. The fact that one has felt at times vaguely lecherous about one's aunt is neither here nor there. Perhaps I'll go back to London tonight after all.

'Cynthia, I am thinking that perhaps I might go back to London after all, as the others are going.'

'Of course, Philip. Do just as you like. Lord Tamworth is showing up my ignorance about books. I haven't read any-thing new. I wish you would talk to him instead.'

She knows. She gave herself away, she wouldn't have spoken so coolly as that if she hadn't minded. She wouldn't have spoken so coolly as that a week or two ago either. She knows.

Bringing his conversation with Lord Tamworth to a barely polite close, he followed her, caught her up on her way across the lawn towards a group in which Aylmer was talking, and said, 'It was because I thought it wasn't safe for us to be left alone together that I said that.'

'Safe?'

'You are married and I am your nephew.'

'That exactly makes us safe. What do you mean, Philip? Are you teasing?'

'No.'

They had reached the group, and were obliged to join in its conversation.

Cynthia thought that Philip was joking. All the same, she found herself asking Aylmer to stay.

'Of course I will if you want me to. But I've made all my arrangements, that's the trouble. And it's awfully short notice to cancel the meeting. I suppose I could telephone tonight and see if they could change it. I don't know whether they'll be able to, though, they're all busy people.'

'It doesn't matter really. It was just an idea.'

'I think in a way, unless you feel very strongly about it, I ought to stick to my original plan. It seems rather inconsiderate to the others, don't you know?'

'Of course. I only meant, if it didn't make any difference.'

'That's all right then. I'm sorry about being so busy lately, I'm looking forward to our holiday, aren't you?'

'Yes.'

She had a busy life, too, days full of engagements of one sort or another. Lately he had felt that she was not as contented as usual; but in the summer recess they would sort it all out, iron out the little differences, give all their time to each other. That was what he wanted to do. He knew she understood.

'It won't be long now.'

'I know.' She turned away. She had to give her attention to her guests.

Alice saw them gathering together to see Violet and Wilfred leave. Cynthia, who had been upstairs to see if Violet was ready, came down smiling. Kitty followed her. Edmund stood by his father at the foot of the stairs, looking up. Alice thought how alike they all looked, except for Philip, who had gone to stand beside Cynthia.

Then Violet came down, followed by Wilfred, and everyone clapped and called out to them, and they kissed their parents, and made their way slowly towards the door, and climbed into the Silver Wraith which was waiting there, with Moberley at the wheel, to take them to the station. Mrs. Weston had insisted that they should go in her car. She said it was so much nicer than Aylmer's, which was true.

And they waved, and drove off, and everybody waved and smiled and called out, 'Good-bye, good-bye', and Cynthia waved and smiled rather tearfully until they were out of sight, and then sighed, and, turning to Philip who was nearest to her, said, 'Well, it is all over now.'

121

Chapter Seventeen

Before dinner, Cynthia rested on her bed. She was a little tired after the wedding, but happy, because it had gone so well.

She lay on her back, wrapped in her Chinese dressing-gown. Her bedroom windows were open, the curtains moving slightly in the warm breeze.

She thought of her hands, in order to relax them, then of her arms, neck, head, torso, legs, feet, until at last like music which may convey nothing until unexpectedly one slips into the pattern of it, the rhythm of her own resting body took her and she floated, in submission.

A long time passed. She almost slept but did not sleep.

At last she moved, turned, pressed her face into the pillow, stretched, crossed her arms over her bosom, hands on shoulders, hugging herself smiling. She said, 'Philip Philip Philip!' Like a cat with the cream.

Then she dressed, slowly. She liked dressing. She went down to dinner.

She had not yet had one consciously adulterous thought.

Chapter Eighteen

Cynthia wore her green tea-gown. Philip had changed into a dark-blue smoking jacket.

Old Mrs. Weston had a light meal upstairs on a tray. Kitty and Alice had their supper in the schoolroom, as usual.

They left the curtains undrawn because of the sweet dusk, but needed to light the candles. They talked agreeably, two people charmed by one another.

After dinner she said, 'I think I'll go up.'

'Oh no, it's much too early, you can't be tired.'

'I'm not exactly tired. But it's been a long day. Will you do the lights?'

'Yes. But I wish you wouldn't go.'

'Good night.'

She wasn't tired. She had left him because of some sort of feeling that the evening couldn't last, that it might go wrong, that . . . she didn't know how, but felt it might have gone wrong. She felt that because her relationship with Philip was so extraordinarily precious to her she had to take care of it; and the closeness of that evening, their shared enjoyment of it, the excitement even of the sort of flirtatious tone they sometimes adopted—well, she felt that after dinner it might have gone wrong, he might have grown bored, buried himself in a book, and she might have been disappointed, or she might have said or done something foolish, something which would have spoilt everything, she did not want Philip to know how fond of him she was.

She was sure she had been right to come upstairs. But as she undressed she regretted it. As she sat in her dressing-gown brushing her hair she thought, I might go down again. But she did not go down again.

All the same she did not want to go to bed.

So when she had finished brushing her hair she walked up and down in front of her bedroom windows, the brush still in her hand.

He came in, shutting the door behind him.

'I must talk to you.'

She turned towards him, surprised that he was there, surprised that she was so pleased that he was there.

'I must talk to you.'

She saw that he looked distressed and moved at once towards him.

He embraced her.

His lips on hers were a tremendous shock.

She dropped the hairbrush. Her mouth gave in to his.

She thought, This is impossible. At the same time came the purifying thought. This is Philip, whom I love. But much stronger than that was the deep impulse in her belly which proclaimed her need and therefore, it seemed, her right.

'But Philip, Philip . . .' Soft protestations. Why protest? He consumed them as he kissed her.

They were possessed by passion, fell on to the bed, and made love.

Their act was many acts. Had it had no before or after it would have been only two handsome people on a bed.

She was still in her prime, and healthy; she had fine great breasts and soft skin; even her long lovely throat had hardly a line across it; and he, built on a less grandiose scale, had youth on his side. The first consummation was so quick and violent that it seemed to them as if they had been struck by a thunderbolt. It was only by repeating it that they remembered the details.

It was she who, after the thunderbolt, chose their direction. When they moved, turned, looked at each other, he was frightened; but she could only think of love. Seeing his look, which was one of fear of torment to come, she put her arms round him to comfort him and said, 'Don't speak.' They lay side by side, and he could only feel amazement that she was not angry, and she could only feel gladness and love. He put his hand on her breast, remembering now how he had longed to do that, and bent his head to kiss it slowly; and she turned slightly, fitting her body against his, and they recalled, and repeated more slowly, their former passion; and it was she who said, 'I love you.'

When she slept, she had said no more than that: 'I love you.' He lay awake, wondering what would happen, or what had happened. Then, remembering that Beatrice would come in to call her in the morning, he went back to his own room, leaving Cynthia sleeping.

Chapter Nineteen

Philip got up early and walked round the garden before breakfast. When he came in, he found Kitty and Alice already in the dining-room (it was only their supper which they had in the schoolroom). He helped himself to coffee and scrambled eggs.

'You look gloomy,' said Kitty. 'When are you going back to London?'

'I don't know.'

'Aren't you going today? I wouldn't let them send me away if I'd known you were going to be here.'

'Send you away?'

'We're going to the Tammies, don't you remember?

124

Alice and I. It's because I'm supposed to be pining for Violet.'

'How odd. Why should you pine for Violet?'

'I don't know. It was Enid Tamworth's idea.'

'It was because she thought you might feel an anticlimax after the wedding,' said Alice. 'It was very kind of her.'

'Yes, I know,' said Kitty. 'But it's quite kind of us too because she's got an ugly French relation there that she can't think what to do with, and we're to have conversation lessons and tell each other about our customs.'

'I remember hearing something about it,' said Philip. 'A female relation, isn't that it?'

'She's called Berthe,' said Kitty. 'Berthe aux Grands Pieds. Oh Mother, fancy you coming down to breakfast.'

'I felt so well this morning that I thought I would. Good morning, Miss Benedict. Good morning, Philip.'

Philip jumped up quickly and went to the sideboard saying, 'I'll get you some coffee.'

Cynthia sat down. She looked well, in some sort of pale muslin. She smiled at Philip as he gave her her coffee, a smile which seemed absolutely as usual.

He had not expected her to be so cool. He admired her, feeling himself quite incapable of matching her assurance. At the same time he was intrigued to know what she would say when they were next alone together. She would surely not pretend that nothing had happened? But nothing she did now would surprise him; or perhaps, rather, everything would.

Kitty and Alice had to be embarked. It seemed to take most of the morning. When they had left, Cynthia walked into the garden, and after a few minutes Philip followed her. She was taking the dead heads off the rose-bushes. Philip stood on the lawn watching her.

'What shall we do?' he asked finally.

'I don't know,' she answered.

'Shall I go back to London?'

'Could you—not?' she said, bending over a rose-bush.

'I suppose I could telephone.'

She said nothing.

'When is . . . ?' he began. 'When are they all coming back, the others?'

'On Friday.'

'Would you like me to stay?'

125

She was dropping the dead roses on the ground as she walked through the rose-bed. 'It's as you like,' she said. Then she said, 'I must go and see how Mama is,' and went back into the house.

He sent a telegram to Horgan saying that he was ill but that he would telephone later in the day. He had to do something about Aylmer's shares.

Mrs. Weston came down to lunch, and they talked about the wedding again.

After lunch Cynthia went up to her room to rest.

She was not yet lying down when he came in. They embraced. Then they began to laugh.

He held her away from him, his hands on her shoulders, and they looked at each other and laughed. Why? They did not really know. Pleasure in each other? Release of the tension which had mounted all day? Or were they laughing at themselves for being made ridiculous by their physical desires? They were not laughing at Aylmer. Or was it in fact just that that it did amount to? They did not know. And all their week of love they did not know, or ask.

They had a week, because Aylmer did not come down for the week-end because he was too busy doing preliminary work for the Buckingham Palace conference, and Edmund did not come because he had managed to get himself asked to stay with the Tamworths, where Kitty and Alice were; so they were alone except for old Mrs. Weston, who spent most of the time in her own rooms in another part of the house.

Cynthia had been going to London, where she had several engagements. She sent messages to say she was not coming. No one was surprised. It was supposed that she was worn out after the wedding which had come, after all, in the middle of such a busy season.

Aylmer sent her a note: 'My dear, I think you are quite right to stay there and rest. How I wish I were with you. London is intolerable in this heat. I hope to be able to get away early on Thursday. Things are very exciting here at the moment. No time for more, but all news when I see you. All my love, Aylmer.'

His writing reminded her of him. She spent the morning his letter came at her desk, doing the household accounts; but by the afternoon she was back in her dream of Philip.

Because it was a sort of dream. A dream of love, simplicity and physical joy. She was able to sustain it by telling herself that she loved Philip. She had always loved him; and by a sort of ruthless simplicity she would not allow the shock of discovering that that love involved also physical desire to change its nature. She had loved him for years and now at last she knew him. She had a husband and a duty to her husband, but he was away, and when he came back she would return to being only his wife, and her physical relationship with Philip would have to stop. This was how she saw it in the rare moments when she allowed herself to think. Aylmer was away and would never know, and in the meantime what was impelling her was her love for Philip, a love she never concealed and which had never been incompatible with her love and respect for Aylmer.

The way in which she adapted herself to the new situation was amazing to Philip. She lost none of her assurance of her shining appearance of being at peace with her conscience. She set out on their adventure as if it were a picnic, wearing a pretty dress, smiling because the sun was out.

Their days were spent in walking or reading, or expeditions about the surrounding countryside. Occasionally old Mrs. Weston joined them, but not often, because her rheumatism was bad and she had sunk into one of her moods of depression. At night, or sometimes in the afternoon when Cynthia had her rest, they made love.

Their love-making was passionate. It was different from anything she had ever experienced with Aylmer, because Aylmer had always thought of the sex appetite as a male one. Was it Lord Curzon who was supposed to have said, 'Ladies don't move?' Aylmer would have agreed. Ladies, as opposed to professionals, did not move. They submitted out of the generosity of their sublime natures to the regrettably gross, though natural, desires of gentlemen. Cynthia had more or less fallen in with this view. She was not very observant of her own emotions, nor even very good at recognizing what they were when she did observe them; nor had she the sort of relationship with Aylmer in which such things could be discussed with freedom. So that with Philip she discovered deeper delights than ever before. It made her feel extremely well and happy. Her happiness was of an immediate nature, and even the fact, of which she must have been aware, that it

127

could not last, did not mar it. Her sense of physical well-being made her feel morally in the right.

Philip was less happy. Unlike Cynthia, he could not fit the experience which he was undergoing into his scheme of ideas, and, besides, he felt guilty about neglecting his office. His feelings towards Aylmer were a great deal more complicated than Cynthia's were. In a way he loved Aylmer; he wanted to *be* Aylmer, and suffered from knowing that he never could be Aylmer: at the same time he felt that Aylmer was his enemy, and he wanted to undo him: at the same time again he felt that Aylmer was meet to be despised, and could not altogether despise him. So that there was an aspect of Cynthia to him in which she appeared just as Aylmer's wife. It was perhaps when she was in this aspect that when they were making love he seized her head in both his hands and forced it down between his thighs. But she always met him with her love. If there was anything at all which would give him pleasure she would in the service of love perform it. There was enough of the old relationship left for her to be able to spoil him. He became increasingly enthralled by her.

It was hot. A light haze of heat lay over the garden. Time crept, softpawed. Mrs. Weston lurked, in black, behind the roses, but emerging only smiled and sent for Moberley, who took her off for another shaded drive. In the house the blinds were drawn, dust danced in the shafted sunlight, clocks ticked, feet on the stairs brought only another bowl of roses. The servants moved more slowly because of the heat and the relative lightness of their work, so many of the family being away. Talk of the weather and the village cricket match. Ellen's eighteenth summer. Cynthia's forty-second.

Mrs. Weston, shrouded in chiffon scarves, spoke into the speaking tube about the abyss. It was opening, she said.

'We have to cling to love,' she said. 'Our one talent, the shaping spirit of our imagination, our one hope. And we have hardly even tried to find out what it is. And why should they learn to wield it, these young things I now find all my interest in, these favoured children, Edmund, Alice, Kitty, Violet, Wilfred? Everything is on their side, circumstances are with them, even history might fall in behind them. But if they have any idea of what it is, this love, they should have done something about it already, they should be telling the world now, while they have time, while the world will listen to them and before they cease to matter. They don't know how to. Perhaps their fathers have not told them. Perhaps they will die with their little piece of half-knowledge undeclared, even to themselves, spilt on the sand. Or is it like most messages, incomprehensible except to those who know it already? Well, you see, it is only in old age that the search for sanctions becomes all-absorbing. In youth there are so many distractions. But your eyes change, you have to hold your book at arm's length in order to be able to read it, and substances change, colours are sometimes brighter and sometimes darker, and you get this strange clarity of distance, men walking down a road a long way off, in the sun, between the trees, not knowing why they are going; they are as clear to me as the printed word held at arm's length. The world on a summer afternoon, think of it, Moberley, think of it, doesn't it make your head swim, don't you find the abyss opening under your feet?'

He hadn't listened to a word. He hadn't so much been thinking of something else as of nothing. Nothing much anyway. Concentrating on keeping in tune with the engine, enjoying the sun. He nodded gravely, but it didn't seem to be enough, so he said, 'There's evil about certainly,' a phrase which he found useful.

'Love conquers evil,' she said. 'I wouldn't say it had been proved.'

They joined the main road. They liked the main road and confidently ignored the twenty-miles-an-hour speed-limit, knowing that when the local police saw the Silver Wraith hurtling down the straight before the Charleswood turning, they said respectfully, 'There goes old Mrs. Weston'. She leant forward. 'Let's see if we can beat sixty,' she said. It was their record so far.

One evening Philip made a scene and broke some things.

He had been talking to Horgan on the telephone. Horgan had told him that he had sold Aylmer's and Edmund's shares at last. They had gone down from 42s., at which price Aylmer had bought them, to 2s. Aylmer had lost nearly £9,000. Edmund £3,000. They did not yet know, but must know within a day or two when they had to sign the transfers. It was the second time that week that Philip had telephoned Horgan, but if he had been in the office himself he could probably have got rid of the shares a little earlier, so that the losses would have been slightly less.

'You know what I feel about it,' he said to Horgan, 'and what a nasty position I'm going to be in when they find out. To be frank, I'm relying on you to find me some way of making a bit of it back. I'm simply relying on your help. I've got to, but I think I'm right to do it. You know you owe me something for having helped you in the way I did, though I knew I was running a risk, and I know you won't forget it.'

'Sure, boy, sure, don't worry. Get back to the office as quick as you can and we'll see what we can do. I'm full of schemes. We'll have a night out and talk about it thoroughly. I've got a new girl I want you to meet. Just you throw off that flu germ and get back here and we'll get things moving.'

A night out and a new girl sounded most unlike Horgan, who usually went quietly home to his hotel after working late at his office and had never in Philip's hearing spoken of girls at all. He ought really to be there in the office keeping an eye on him.

Philip thought. A man does not like to feel tied. Besides, there is the future. I am temporarily infatuated, but it will not last. What does she expect? What of Aylmer? And I have to go back to the office, and Horgan. I shall let all that slip through my fingers if I don't. Women don't understand these things. I must get back to Horgan. He is normal. That is real life. Not this. A man does not like to feel tied. But as he thought all this he thought at the same time of Cynthia, simply of her presence, and was confounded.

But he said to her that night, 'I must go back.'

He was standing by her dressing-table. She was in bed. He had just come in, in his silk dressing-gown.

'I know,' she said soothingly. She held a book on her knees. It was *Travels with a Donkey*. Stevenson was her favourite author.

'You are not paying attention,' he said irritably.

'But of course I am. I know you must go back. But must we talk about it?'

'Don't you mind?'

'Yes, I mind.'

'You don't seem to.'

'I only mean, we mustn't panic. Please, Philip, don't think about disagreeable things.'

'I don't understand how you can say that.'

'Why are you so cross?'

'You don't love me.'

'Philip.'

'You don't. Or you couldn't be so calm about it. You're beginning to feel you want to get rid of me.'

'My dear. Nothing could be more wrong. You know that.'

'It isn't wrong. You're tired of me. It was just a temporary infatuation. You wanted a young man, because Aylmer didn't satisfy you, isn't that it?'

'Why are you trying to be destructive? Did you tear off butterflies' wings when you were a little boy?'

'You know perfectly well what I did when I was a little boy.'

'Not when you were a very little boy. You were eight when I first saw you. You had a brown skin and bright light eyes. You looked much healthier then than you do now.'

'I probably was healthier. I had not been civilized.'

'There is nothing wrong with being civilized, is there?'

'Civilization is foul.'

'Not as foul as non-civilization. I didn't know you were a romantic.'

'I am not. I am the opposite of a romantic. Romanticism is lies. It is you who are a romantic. You romanticize us. We need it, that I grant you.'

'I don't think I do. I don't mean to. I feel everything that I say I feel. Surely you believe that?'

'I don't know what to believe. I want to go.'

'Then of course you must.'

'And never see you again?'

'Well, but we shall meet surely,' she said rather hesitantly. 'I mean, in the family, and—this is your home after all.'

'I didn't mean that.'

'Could we not . . . meet . . . in London?'

'You would do that?'

'Yes. I think so.'

'What about Aylmer?'

'I don't know. I love you. But why do we have to think about all this now?'

'It won't get any easier if we put it off. We meet in London then. How often? Mondays and Thursdays do you think? From 5 o'clock till 6 in a room in Pimlico?'

'Don't.'

'You would do this?'

'If you wanted me to, I think I would.'

'Is that the sort of example a mother should set her son?'

'You are not my son.'

'You used to be for ever telling me that I was. I suppose that was self-defence.'

'Why have you turned like this? What has gone wrong? We were so happy, I thought. And as for what I was always telling you, *you* were always telling *me* to change, and not do things in self-defence, and not pretend with you. I have done what you wanted. You said it was what you wanted.'

'Now you blame me. You say it is all my fault. It's not fair.' He was very angry. 'I didn't want you to change. I wanted to be your husband, that's all, I didn't want to have you twice a week in a hired room in . . . You didn't understand, you're too crude, I wanted . . . not that. And now it's too late. You're my mistress, I'm your lover, for ever and ever. For ever and ever, do you see?'

She only gazed at him.

'Don't you see what you have done?' he shouted.

'What I have done?' she repeated. 'But you have done it.'

'No!' Furiously, he swept his arm across her dressing-table. The mirror crashed to the ground, with all her little boxes and pretty bottles strewn around it. He stamped on it and it splintered. He shouted again, 'I didn't want to know that what I guessed was true . . . Don't you see?'

'But you made it true,' she said. 'By believing it.'

'What are you saying? It's not my fault. Have I got to bear all the guilt as well as everything else? What are you doing to me?'

'I am not doing anything. Please be reasonable. Come here and sit down.'

He sat down on her bed, leaving the wreckage. She held

his hand, and they remained in silence. At last she lifted his hand and kissed it gently.

'Cynthia.' He held her face in both of his hands and gazed at it, saying, 'I love you, I love you, I love you.'

Beatrice found them the next morning when she came to call Cynthia, their dark heads turned away from each other on the pillow, their bodies, lightly covered by a sheet and a blanket, not touching any more, but resting. The other bedclothes were on the floor. So was the wreckage from the dressing-table.

Beatrice shut the door quickly.

The click of the handle woke Philip, who got up and went back to his own room.

Half an hour later Beatrice called Cynthia.

Cynthia, stretching, said, 'Oh, Beatrice, the wind or something . . . I wonder if you'd mind clearing up the mess?'

Chapter Twenty

House of Commons,
S.W.
14th July, 1914

My dear,

All well here.

Scene in the library on a hot summer afternoon: three Tory Members fast asleep, their round red faces raised to heaven snoring their thanks for their good lunch, a worthy Lib-Lab battling with the books of reference, seeking stuff with which later on to sweep the three good Tories' foundations from under their feet (he thinks), an Irish Member glowering at the *Pink 'Un*, and a mild middle-aged Liberal with a perpetually puzzled frown (it's the ways of man, you see, that baffle him) sitting in a corner, writing to his wife.

We have been working furiously for this conference. The other people concerned are Asquith and Lloyd George for our side, Bonar Law and Landsdowne for the Tories, Carson and Craig for Ulster and Redmond and Dillon for the Nationalists. From our preliminary work I would say there may be a good chance of success. It would be gratifying, wouldn't it, to get this tedious problem out of the way before the summer recess? The general tone is still far too quarrelsome, and Carson no less ludicrously autocratic, but I think there are enough men of goodwill to prevail. I hope to slip away early on Thursday so as to have a decent week-end for once. Reggie seemed to think they might like to come over on Sunday.

It has been hot. I have thought of you under the weeping ash. The international situation is improving. It seems as though Serbia will accept Austria's ultimatum, severe though the terms of it were. And so another little crisis is survived. It is unreal somehow—no one in their right mind wants war, and yet we progress from crisis to crisis—but no one *does* want war, for even the most puffed-up Prussian is not a madman, and the modern financial set-up is such that we should all, friend and foe alike, be bankrupt after a few weeks of war. But peace, which seems such a simple affair, is cruelly complicated after all.

I saw Tammy for a moment at the Club. He said Kitty had charmed everybody and been very amusing and pretty. They were also delighted my our Miss Benedict, and said she was a quite exceptional personality. I am inclined to agree. And then, walking back to the House from the Club, across the park, I ran into Ida and a whole collection of her friends on their way back from some good work or other, wearing their charity hats, very sweet and high-spirited. She reminded me about the last time she came to stay and about how we played—apparently, though I must confess I had forgotten all about it—some sort of statue game. Anyway she hailed me as Goodwill personified, rather to the others' surprise. You, it seems, were the very meaning and essence of life itself—a heavy role.

That was what I had to tell you, then, that I hope to be home on Thursday, in time for tea, and that I hope to find you very well, and quite rested, and ready for some long walks with

your loving
Aylmer

Chapter Twenty-one

Philip returned to London on Wednesday night. Cynthia had begged him to stay and to be there when Aylmer arrived. She had said, 'It will be easier. We shall get it over. When we are all together we shall remember how fond we are of him and he will be the same as ever and there will be nothing to worry about.' But Philip would not stay. 'I'll come back on Friday,' he said, 'with Edmund. We'll come together, and Kitty will be back by then, and it will be just the usual sort of family thing. That will make it easier.'

Privately he thought he might not come back, out of cowardice, but that was on Wednesday. On Friday he telephoned Edmund and arranged to travel down with him.

He found him waiting for him on the platform at Paddington. Edmund had changed into his country clothes, a light Prince of Wales suit, a soft hat and suède shoes; a correct and pleasing figure, solid amid the encircling steam of Paddington.

'I've got seats. It looks as if we may have the carriage to ourselves,' he said.

Philip saw at once that something was wrong. The frank gaze of the blue eyes was withheld. Philip felt suddenly a little frightened. Edmund's disapproval could be very chilling. It's the money, he thought. It was.

'I was sent a rather worrying document this morning,' said Edmund, after the train had pulled out of the station and it had become clear that they were indeed the only people in the carriage.

'Oh dear,' said Philip.

'It was about my Cape Enterprise shares,' said Edmund.

'Ah,' said Philip. 'I had hoped to have a chance to talk to you about that before they sent you the transfers.'

'I suppose there was some mistake?' said Edmund. 'I mean according to what I received this morning I've lost £3,000.'

'It's been a failure, I'm afraid. I do feel extremely embarrassed about it, which was why I was hoping to be able to talk to you about it first. As you know, I said a week ago that I would sell Aylmer's and your shares as soon as I could and for as fair a price as I could get, and that we

135

should have to regard it as a failure and cut our losses and hope to do better next time.'

'Next time?' repeated Edmund, with a certain blankness.

'I do of course regard it as my responsibility. I thought we were on to a good thing, you see, and I was quite simply wrong. But I know a little more about this business now and I'm determined to find another investment which really will fructify.'

'You mean you want us to give you some more money?'

'I mean that I want to find a really good investment for you.'

'But I can't afford another investment. Look here, Philip, I don't think you realize quite how serious this is. How much has Father lost?'

'About £9,000. I do realize how serious it is.'

'£9,000. But he can't afford it. He simply can't. We shall have to start selling or we shall be in bad trouble. I shall have to arrange it tomorrow. Does Father know?'

'Not yet.'

'I thought not. He's even more hopeless about that sort of thing than I am. Look here, old boy, I know this is bad luck on you, but do you realize your wretched schemes are going to force us to break up the estate, sell land we've owned for hundreds of years? We'll have to sell at least one farm.'

'Please don't do that without going into the whole thing very carefully. It would be much better to borrow. And there is this new scheme of Horgan's, which is quite a different affair.'

'I am not going to the money-lenders.'

'I mean the bank.'

'Both of us already have bank loans. And as for new schemes of your friend Horgan . . . No, no, Philip, this is a very bad business. Have you lost money too?'

'A little. But my investment was smaller.'

'And Mother?'

'Very little.'

'At least one is supposed to enjoy gambling in the ordinary way. But this way seems to have no advantages whatsoever.'

'I wish you would believe me when I say I mean to make it up.'

'How?'

'By the opposite process.'

'We can't let you experiment with our money any more or we shall have none left. And you haven't any of your own.'

'I shall make it. You may sneer at Horgan's schemes, but this one is going to make a great deal of money. It is a speculation in property. He has bought . . .'

'I don't want to know,' Edmund stood up abruptly. 'No, I'm sorry about this, Philip. I'll write it off as money given to you to get you going in what you want to do. And so will Father, I feel sure. And he will do it with a far better grace than I can because he is a far better person. I'm going along to get a drink.'

'I'm sorry,' said Philip, rather loudly. 'What more can I say except that I'm sorry? I won't say this again, but you will see that I will make it up one day before very long. But I fully agree with you that the whole business is quite simply bloody.'

Edmund turned, sat down again in the corner opposite to Philip.

'I know,' he said. He sat in silence, feeling his anger against Philip slowly dissipating. 'I dare say the same thing would have happened to me,' he said after a time. But as soon as he had said it they both realized that it was not true. Edmund had always been more competent than Philip. But without giving the thought time to feed his bitterness, Edmund went on, 'You see, it's come at a very bad time for me. I was thinking of getting married.'

Philip only groaned slightly. Everything was going very very badly indeed.

After a time he said, 'Would you do one thing? I have a slight problem with Aylmer, that is to say I want to have a day, just a day, with Aylmer before he knows about this thing. They'll have sent the transfers to his London address, so he won't have got them and he needn't know till you tell him. Otherwise it will be impossible, I can't explain why but I'll never be able to speak to him again unless I have just one day, one ordinary day with him, before he finds out. Could you do that? It's terribly important.'

'I ought to discuss it with him tomorrow so that we can decide what step to take.'

'Please. It's almost a matter of life and death. I can't tell you why but please wait for a day.'

'I suppose it would spoil his week-end. I could try and leave it till the next day.'

'Thank you. It would mean a great deal to me.'

'I think I'll go and get that drink.'

Philip sat alone in the carriage watching the passing country-side. After a time he thought, They were fools to trust me with the money in the first place.

It was not quite a whole day in the end.

There was Friday evening. Everything seemed as usual. Absurdly so. There were a few young people staying: they had arrived earlier by car. Cynthia looked beautiful, was perhaps a little quieter than usual. So was Edmund, though Philip seemed in lively form. Aylmer was benign, at the head of the table, smiling at the conversation, encouraging the younger ones to talk; a typical Friday evening. And after dinner they walked in the garden a little because it was such a beautiful evening, and Philip and Cynthia walked side by side and he said, 'I am very unhappy,' and she said, 'It's too difficult, I don't know what we are all meant to do.'

'I must see you,' he said.

'Next week, in London.'

'Is he all right?'

'Yes, yes. Everything is the same as usual. Except that I am in love.'

'I know. I am in love too.'

Aylmer was walking with his mother down to the particular garden bench where she sat to feed her two tame squirrels; and they were there, even though it was beginning to grow dark. Aylmer went back to the house to get food for them and passed Cynthia and Philip on the way.

'You look sad, you two,' he said. 'Come and see the squirrels, I am going to get food for them.'

They began to walk down towards the bench.

'It will be all right,' said Cynthia.

But after lunch the next day Beatrice asked to see Aylmer.

I have sometimes thought that but for Beatrice everything might have been all right. Nothing might have happened. Because that is one of the things about grown-up life: there are situations, people poised, something has been set in motion, and then, somehow, nothing happens; time passes, the situation dissipates into a hundred little sidelines, the people move, change, disappear, and nothing really after all has happened: it has just been another moment in a shifting pattern, a particularly complex grouping of objects, having as far as one can tell no meaning at all.

But I may be wrong about Beatrice, because hers was a very minor role. She was only the agent, and there are always agents.

So here is Beatrice with her yellow face, confronting Aylmer across his desk. He is wearing a cricket shirt, open at the neck, and grey flannel trousers held up rather bunchily by an ancient leather belt; she is in her dark uniform, cuffs, cap and all. On this yellow face is malevolence, self-righteousness, prudery, lasciviousness, and pride: the combination is ghastly. She is suffering, poor woman, but she is very unpleasant all the same.

Aylmer smiles politely, thinking Good God, the woman must be ill.

'Yes, Beatrice?'

Holding a green glass paperweight comfortably in his hand, a good lunch just over, a summer afternoon outside, his books, his family, his country, his duty, his hopes. 'Yes, Beatrice?' Afterwards he will walk down to the river: the children were talking of bathing. He will walk down with Cynthia to see them, looking at the roses on the way.

'I wish to give notice, Sir Aylmer.'

'Oh dear, Beatrice, I am very sorry to hear that. Have you spoken to Her Ladyship about it?'

'No, Sir Aylmer. I thought it best to come to you.'

'I see. Well, as you know, she usually deals with these things, and no doubt if there was some little difficulty which could be sorted out she'd be the best person to help you. But if you've definitely made up your mind . . .'

'There was a particular reason why I preferred to come to you, Sir Aylmer. The reason for my giving in my notice has to do with Her Ladyship herself. There have been goings on.'

'Oh really? Oh well, let's not go into it, Beatrice. Let's just say that . . .'

'Such as I am not used to.'

'Quite. Yes. I'm sorry to hear it.'

'I have seen a lot of things in my time and felt it my duty to make no mention of it. But this is something different. I couldn't stay in such a house, Sir Aylmer, not with things like that going on. It's sin, outright sin. Such as I am not used to.'

'Yes, I see. Well, Beatrice, if you've made up your mind . . .'

'Nor would you wish to condone it, Sir Aylmer, that I am sure of. They should be punished for it, as they will be in afterlife, that I do know. But I couldn't stay with that going on. I nearly packed my bags there and then, when I found them. But then I thought it my duty to stay and see you. Found them there sleeping, I did, in the broad daylight in the morning. Naked but for a sheet, the two of them, and all the room upside down. And if that isn't sin I don't know what is. Her and her own nephew that we all thought was like a son to her. Not but what I've had my suspicions. You get to know when you've suffered a bit yourself, you get an eye for treachery.'

'Beatrice, I don't quite know what you are saying, but I think you are unwise to excite yourself. I think it would be best if I just accepted your notice and we left it at that.'

'It's as you wish, Sir Aylmer. It's nothing to do with me. It's not my affair. If you think you can leave it at that with a thing like that going on in your own family, with your wife deceiving you with your nephew every time you turn your back, well and good, that's what I say. It's no concern of mine, that's what I say.'

'Please leave.'

'I am only trying to do my duty, Sir Aylmer. I wanted to go there and then, as I said, but I thought, having been in the family all these years, I thought, I can't let him go on in ignorance, I thought.'

'I have asked you to leave. I accept your notice and I should be glad if you would be out of the house in an hour's time.'

'Of course it is impossible to expect gratitude, that I do realize. You don't expect gratitude when you have seen as much of people as I have. But to be turned out of the house without so much as . . .'

'Get out. Or I shall ring for James to carry you out. And then go away. If you are not out of the house by 4 o'clock I shall send for the police.'

Cynthia was resting when Aylmer went to find her. She usually lay on her bed for half an hour or so after lunch and often went to sleep, but today she was awake.

Aylmer came in and said, 'Rather a beastly thing has happened.'

She sat up. 'I can see it has. Tell me quickly what it is.'

He sat down on the edge of her bed. 'Beatrice came to see me. To give her notice.'

'That's not a beastly thing. It's rather a good thing. She's been very peculiar lately.'

'I know. I think that's what it was really. But she said some extraordinarily unpleasant things.'

'Poor Aylmer. How horrid for you. Why did she go to you and not to me?'

'Well, that's the trouble, you see. The unpleasant things were about you.'

'Were they indeed? The old beast. Never mind, don't tell me, it will only annoy me. I suppose I have been rather sharp with her lately, but she has been so forgetful.'

'She seemed to be trying to tell me something about you and Philip. I didn't want to listen.'

Cynthia had been sitting up in bed. Now she turned and slid out from under the covers. She had taken off only her shoes and these she now put on, bending over them, one hand on the bed. Then she walked to her dressing-table and began to rearrange her hair, standing in front of the mirror she had bought to replace the one which Philip had broken.

'What did she say?'

'She's obviously completely twisted. I shut her up immediately, of course. I've told her to be out of the house within an hour.'

'What did she say?'

'She said she had found you both in here when she came to call you one morning. She said you were both in the bed.'

141

Cynthia stopped combing her hair. After a moment she turned towards Aylmer and looked at him. He returned her glance apologetically.

She said, 'I can't tell you how glad I am that Beatrice said that.'

'What?'

'I have been wanting to talk to you about it.'

'What?'

'I need your help, Aylmer. Please help me, as you always do.'

'Of course.' He was totally at a loss. She looked so serious that he had an idea that it might be something to do with money.

'This thing with Philip,' she said. 'I am in such trouble about it, and I am so thankful to think that now you will know about it and be able to help me.' She sat down on a chair facing him, her hands clasped on her lap. 'I have been in such a muddle.'

He merely nodded.

She went on. 'It seemed so simple. There was so much love, you see. And also there was the fact that I knew such things did exist in other people's lives and didn't make them stop being what they were, you know what I mean? But then when you came back it all changed. You remember the night you came back and I couldn't sleep and walked about in the garden half the night? I was thinking about it, you see, having not allowed myself to think about it before. I was realizing that it was a treacherous thing to have done, and that there weren't any excuses after all. Can you see at all how it happened?'

He looked as though he had become several stones heavier, staring at her from the edge of her bed. 'I'm sorry. I just don't know what you are talking about.'

Her face was smooth with the calm of confession.

'You know how much I have always loved him, and how it had never interfered in the least with what I feel for you. I let that mislead me. I suppose I didn't understand my own emotions. But, you see, I have never had to distrust my own emotions before. I have always thought it was perfectly safe and right to follow them. But I see now that it was wrong, quite wrong. That is why I want you to know all about it. So that you can help me, so that we can

142

see that no harm comes of it. But you will have to help me. Because I still have the emotions. I mean I have them worse than ever. You will help me?'

'But how?'

'I mean, keep me safe, from Philip.'

He frowned heavily. 'You mean, he has been bothering you?'

'You haven't understood at all.' She clasped her hands more firmly together. 'Please, Aylmer, try to understand. I am in trouble, don't you see? I am in love with him. I can't help it. But I want to do the right thing. I want you to help me.'

'In love with whom?'

'With Philip.'

'You are in love with Philip,' he repeated dully.

'But I want you to help me. And to help him. If I had known I would never have done it. I didn't know what it would mean.'

'What what would mean?'

'What we did. It seemed so simple.'

He shut his eyes for a moment. Then he said, 'You mean that Beatrice's story was true?'

'Yes. That's why I need your help, you see.'

'But that was incest,' he said.

'Incest?' She looked surprised.

'Yes. He's your nephew.'

'Oh, but . . . by marriage only.'

'It doesn't matter. You are his father's brother's wife.'

'Oh.'

'It is incest.'

They sat in silence until she said, tentatively, 'Does it matter what name we call it?'

'It is not a question of calling it a name,' he said in his heavy voice. 'It is incest.'

'Yes, I see. But not a—well, what I mean is, not a very *close* sort of incest, surely?'

'It doesn't matter,' he said. 'It is still incest.'

Now it was she who looked baffled.

'In my own family,' he said.

'I don't ask you to forgive me or anything like that,' she said. 'Only to help me, to help us all.'

He stared at her.

'Incest is committed by the lower classes in remote country districts,' he said without expression.

'Aylmer . . .' she appealed.

'It is impossible.' He stood up and beat his hands together. 'It is impossible, impossible. Tell me it is not true.'

She only looked at him with concern.

'Philip. Ah.' He gave a sort of low intermittent shout. It was the noise that Members of Parliament make during each other's speeches, a sort of 'row row row row row'. Then he said, 'Philip. I'll find him, I'll . . .' and went to the door.

'Aylmer, please, this is all wrong.' She ran after him and took his arm.

'Don't touch me!' he said, scraping the words up through his throat.

He pulled the door open and rushed down the stairs.

We were all sitting in the drawing-room, where we had gone after lunch for a quiet hour or so before beginning more energetic amusements. Philip was reading in an armchair, Edmund talking in a desultory way about shooting to one of the young men, the rest of us sewing or reading or talking quietly..

Aylmer burst in. He looked most terribly ill. None of us had ever seen him look like that before. He went up quite close to Philip and stood looking down at him, and trying to speak.

'You have . . . you have . . .' he began.

Philip did not move, and after one startled look at him turned his eyes back towards his book as if he were reading. His face went a sort of yellowish colour.

Then Aylmer, failing to speak, turned and walked heavily out into the garden. Edmund was going to follow him, but by that time Cynthia had come in and she restrained him, putting her hand on his arm and saying, 'No, Edmund. It would be better to leave him alone for a little.'

So we left him alone.

And in the evening Kitty found him dead in the river, floating face downward in the pool where she had gone to swim.

Chapter Twenty-two

Here is Philip in what seems to be a room in Hell. Move a little this way, pushing through the crowd, and you will see him better, through the smoke and the fire-coloured light, dancing violently, with his hair fallen over his white face and his eyes frenzied, possessed by the music: no, desiring to be possessed by the music but not possessed. And he is sweating; that is sweat on the white face, not tears, for though his eyes were watering that is only because of the smoke; and the sweat is understandable because the heat is terrible in this hellish night-club, and he is dancing ragtime with the same ungainly over-enthusiasm with which his grandsons fifty years later throw themselves into the Twist. (He has several grandsons, bright-faced public schoolboys of a now rather outdated type, trusting to their grandfather's name to get them jobs in Lloyds or a decent firm of stockbrokers.) But of course he is not driven by their simple love of noisy exercise; it is less than a week since Aylmer died, and Aylmer's death was fairly heavy on his mind for longer than that.

Horgan had a name, James; but even the girl called him Horgan. At least she was hardly a girl, being nearer forty than thirty. She was called Leslie, and lived in a flat in Bayswater with her seven-year-old daughter. She had been more or less bequeathed to Horgan by a former associate of his, a Lebanese import-export man whose companion she had been for some years during his visits to London. This Mr. Harouni used to spend eight months of the year in London and the other four in West Africa with his wife and children. Now in his old age he was handing over his business to his sons and retiring with his wife to the Lebanon. He had suggested to Horgan that the latter might care to take an interest in Leslie because she was likely to be lonely and because he himself would prefer more varied sexual amusements during his now briefer and less frequent stays in London.

Horgan paid the rent of the flat in Bayswater but did not move in there because that would have meant an intimacy of which he was by now temperamentally incapable. He stayed in his hotel, but visited Leslie nearly every evening on his way back from the office. She usually cooked him dinner—she was quite a good cook—and sometimes he took her to a musical show or for a drive in a hired car out into the country. It was as near to regular domesticity as he wished to get; and she made no complaints if he was too busy to see her for several days. The arrangement pleased him.

'A man needs a woman,' he said to Philip. 'A regular woman. Keeps him in trim. But you don't want to waste time and energy messing about chasing them. You want a steady convenient arrangement that's to everyone's advantage. She gets something out of it, I get something out of it. That's good business.'

Philip wondered what they talked about, since he regarded Horgan when it was not a matter of figures as probably the dullest man in England, but when he had seen them together once or twice he understood that they did not exactly converse. She talked about her family, her little girl's exploits at school, her mother's quarrel with her aunt in Manchester, her brother-in-law's stomach troubles; Horgan half-listened, occasionally putting in a sceptical comment on someone's behaviour. When he felt like talking he talked about his business, and Leslie half-listened, occasionally putting in a question to keep him going, or sounding a dutiful note of admiration. They seemed well enough contented with each other.

Philip returned to London immediately after Aylmer's death was discovered. He simply left the house, and in the crisis no one really saw him go. When he went to his office the next morning the papers were already full of the news of the Cabinet Minister's mysterious death, together with the first suggestions of the rumours which soon briefly occupied London—was it accident, suicide, murder? Was it the suffragettes, the Irish, or the prelude to a nasty political scandal?

Horgan said, 'See your uncle kicked the bucket.'

'Yes,' said Philip.

'Bad luck,' said Horgan. 'Nothing to do with politics, was it?'

'No,' said Philip.

Horgan asked no more questions, either then or later. Philip thought at first that it might be delicacy on his part;

146

then he wondered whether it might be embarrassment, because of some idea Horgan might have that Aylmer's losses over Cape Enterprises had contributed to his suicide; later he realized that Horgan asked no questions because he was not interested in knowing the answers. This absence of curiosity about anything not immediately connected with the manipulation of money seemed to Philip marvellous. It was also, for the time being, soothing, and Philip resolved to spend as much of his time as possible with Horgan. He found that by being with him he came to know the workings of his mind, and to admire them for their efficiency and speed. At the same time he saw that Horgan, in spite of his idea of himself as a man who 'thought big', lacked imagination, and this Philip thought should be his own contribution to their association. As his knowledge increased and his suggestions became more useful, he was pleased to notice the adaptability which Horgan displayed, and the ease with which he absorbed Philip's ideas, showing no sign of resentment or offended vanity. This was the beginning of a long partnership.

It was a result, indirectly, of Philip's resolution to devote himself to Horgan and work that he found himself in a night-club. They had had dinner in the Bayswater flat, Horgan, Leslie, and Philip, and after dinner Horgan had suggested that they should all go round to his hotel for a drink; but in the large and ugly hotel bar conversation flagged even more than usual and soon Horgan stood up and said, 'I'm going to bed. See Leslie home like a good chap, would you, Philip? Call in at a night-club on the way, why don't you? I know you know all the night spots, and she doesn't get much excitement with me.'

They demurred, but he said, 'No, no, enjoy yourselves. Here you are.' He handed Philip £1 with some grandeur, and said, 'You needn't stay long.' He waved them off and turned back towards the lifts.

Leslie was not exactly the companion Philip would have chosen, but he was willing enough to defer going to bed. At the back of his mind during all this time was the thought of the telephone ringing in his flat, and not being answered, and the cool voice of the office telephonist saying, 'I'm afraid Mr. Weston is not taking any calls this morning,' which was what he had told her to say whenever Cynthia rang up. He had thoughts of himself as ruthless for some time, but this was in fact the first truly ruthless thing he did. He refused to speak to Cynthia until long afterwards; and as far as I know he never visited Charleswood again.

He wanted to avoid people who knew him, so he took Leslie to Soho. As they walked down the stairs into the smoky basement, she surprised him by saying in a rather affected voice, 'Why, what a divvy place!'

She sat down and looked round her with interest, asked Philip about various of the people who were there, and generally seemed pleased.

'Don't you go out much with Horgan?' he asked.

'Hardly at all. He likes to go to bed early.'

'You don't find that dull?'

'No. I'm used to it. My friend Manou was the same, very quiet.'

'Do you miss him?'

'Manou? Oh yes. But Horgan's very easy, you know. I mean, he doesn't ask much of anybody, does he, outside of business?'

'But does he make you happy?'

She looked at him kindly, and explained, 'You have to take what you can get at my age, and with a daughter to support.'

'Why couldn't you go and live with your family?'

She laughed. 'You don't know my family. I believe you're sentimental.'

'No. I'm just wondering about you.'

'I like sentimental people. Let's talk about you instead. Have you a girl friend?'

'No. I don't believe in regular relationships of that sort. Besides, I like variety. Would you mind if I got drunk?' He was rather drunk already.

'Of course not. It will remind me of my young days. They're quiet-living, these business-men, as I say. It will make a change.'

'I've had rather a shock recently,' he said in excuse.

'Horgan told me about your uncle.'

'Did he? What did he say?'

'That he'd committed suicide, that's all. But I read about it in the papers. It must have been awful for her.'

'For her?'

'Lady Weston. You know, you'll hardly believe this, but she's always been a great hero of mine, or heroine I suppose I should say. I've got ever so many photos of her.'

'Let's dance,' he said.

The place was crowded. He drank rapidly. Once she said to him, 'You'll be sick before the night's out,' like a nanny saying, 'it will end in tears', but her expression remained serene, her general appearance neat and respectable. Her large face was an agreeable squarish shape, and though her complexion was poor her teeth were white and even. He said, 'You must have been quite nice-looking when you were younger.' She took it as easily as she seemed to take everything. 'They used to say so,' she said. 'Oh, yes, I've had my successes.'

He had a period of temporary euphoria, dancing with her. 'This is jolly good fun,' he said.

That state soon passed, and he began to lose touch, faces swirled round him, and he needed all his concentration to keep his equilibrium. Even sitting down he felt it wiser to hold on to the table. And then suddenly there was little Smallpiece's face close to his, little Smallpiece, his erstwhile brother officer, whom he had hardly seen since he had left the Army.

'What are you doing here?' he said.

'Weston! My dear fellow!' And then the joy was clouded. 'But look here, I mean, I say, aren't you . . . ? I mean . . .'

'You think it is too soon after my uncle's death for me to be throwing myself so whole-heartedly into the whirl of London night-life?' said Philip very clearly.

'Well, it did occur to me, old fellow, since you say so.'

'Since after all he was as good as a father to me,' said Philip.

'Quite,' said Smallpiece.

'Quite,' said Philip, nodding several times.

'Oh well, I must be getting back to my table,' said little Smallpiece, evidently embarrassed. He bowed politely to Leslie.

'Captain Smallpiece—Miss . . . er . . .' said Philip rather belatedly.

'Miss Fowler. Pleased to meet you,' said Leslie.

'Look here,' said Smallpiece, turning back to Philip. 'If you want to get back in again any time, just let me know. I mean, into the regiment. Most of our chaps think the war's bound to come now, and you want to get in quick if you don't want to miss it. They all seem to think it's not going to be a long affair. Just let me know, won't you?'

They watched him thread his way neatly back to his table and join an obvious brother officer and two obvious chorus girls, of whom one was tall and one small.

'Which do you think is his, the big one or the little one?' said Philip.

'The big one, I expect,' said Leslie. 'People never choose what's suitable, do they? If my Lucile was a boy I'd be worried.'

'Why?'

'This war business.'

'She'll be all right. She'll be able to be a real twentieth-century woman when she grows up.'

'So there's going to be another new woman. What will she be like, then, poor thing?'

'She'll have much more emancipated ideas about sex.'

'I've had some pretty emancipated ideas about sex myself in my time, and I'm no new woman.'

'I like you,' he said, gripping the table. 'I like you very much.'

'I think it's time I saw you home. Hey, you, let's have the bill, shall we?'

In the cab he insisted that they should go to her flat in Bayswater first. 'I promised Horgan to see you home,' he said, obstinately.

When they arrived he said he would come in with her.

'You could make me some coffee,' he said. 'You will make me some coffee, won't you? It would just sober me up and then I could get home. Not that I'm at all drunk, I just feel drunk.'

The first thing he saw when he went into her sitting-room was a photograph of Cynthia. It was on a postcard on the mantelpiece.

He said, 'What's that? What are you doing with that?' rather aggressively.

'I told you,' she said. 'I've got hundreds of them. You know, there are shops where you can buy them. I've got some of Mrs. Cornwallis West too, but not as many as I have of Lady Weston. Want to see them?'

She pulled out a drawer in a little writing-table.

'Look.' She knelt on the floor and began to lay them out as if she were going to play some sort of game of Patience with them. 'I cut some of them out of the *Tatler* or the newspapers. Look at this one. Isn't it beautiful?'

'I didn't know you could get so many of these things.'

'Of course you can. Some people sue, to stop them being sold, but she wouldn't bother with anything so petty, I shouldn't think. Besides, why not give a bit of innocent pleasure? Isn't that a lovely one, in that hat? I do think she's a wonderful person. You can look at them while I make the coffee.'

He stood swaying and looking down at all the images of Cynthia spread at his feet. I could tread on them, he thought. He remembered the crunch of her bedroom mirror under his feet. The photographs swirled slightly below him as he tried to fix his gaze on them; they seemed to merge, they were a lady in a white dress and a large hat, in a brownish photograph, no more. Fumbling with his buttons, bracing his legs like a pony, he thought he would pee on them.

'Gerroutofit!' It was the sort of cry one would use to a pony that was misbehaving. She took him by the shoulders and pushed him into the lavatory. 'That's the place for that sort of thing.'

Even so she was not shocked. When he came back into the room the photographs had gone, even the one which had been on the mantelpiece, and she was pouring out the coffee.

'I'm sorry,' he said.

'I should think so. Here, drink this.'

'I really am sorry. I am ashamed of myself. I mean, that's what I am. I am not ashamed of being ashamed of myself.'

'I can't think why not. Drink up your coffee, and then you must go home.'

'I am a failure. Things haven't gone at all as I meant them to go.'

But he was too incoherent to be able to communicate with her, and she was not quite interested enough, or perhaps too tired, to try to find out through his drunkenness why he had begun his little gesture. Trying to approach her with vaguely amorous intent, he knocked over a small table, and she said, rather sharply, 'Be careful, you'll wake

Lucile!' But she sent him home quite kindly, patting him on the shoulder and saying, 'You know, you've got a lot to learn.'

He said he would learn it.

And did learn a good deal.

Chapter Twenty-three

It killed old Mrs. Weston. But then she was old and would have died soon anyway.

The day after Aylmer's death she went for a drive with Moberley in the afternoon: she had to, she had so much on her mind, and he was the only person to whom she could talk. It was that morning, early, that she had gone into Cynthia's room and said, 'Was Philip your lover?' and Cynthia, who had just managed to fall asleep for the first time since the death, turned a puffy face deeper into the pillow and said, 'Oh yes, yes,' almost irritably. 'And he found out?' 'Beatrice told him.'

Mrs. Weston stalked on, black-booted, into Edmund's room, where she found him half-dressed, and said to him, 'This is a terrible thing to have to tell you, but I think it right that you should know. Your mother and your cousin Philip were lovers. It was not the money.' And she stalked out again.

All morning she was shut in her room and would speak to no one, though Edmund came to knock on her door several times. She refused lunch, but in the afternoon rang for Moberley and the car.

He drove slowly, avoiding the village, speaking only a little in soothing commonplaces. When she noticed that he had avoided the village she said, 'Why don't you take me through the village? Do you think I am afraid of them?'

He did not answer.

'Do you think I am afraid of them?' she repeated harshly. 'I don't mind being peered at.'

'I thought you might prefer to see the countryside,' he said.

She resented his tact.

'The whole thing's your fault anyway, for behaving so

badly to Beatrice,' she said aggressively. 'If you hadn't treated her like that she would never have turned bitter. She caused all the trouble, did you know that?'

'I'm very sorry to hear that,' he said.

'She went to Sir Aylmer with some terrible stories.'

As if to end the conversation she picked up *The Times* which she had brought with her, and held it at arm's length, frowning at it. She had forgotten to bring her reading glasses. Even so, she seemed to see enough to confirm her worst suspicions. She put down the paper and went on attacking him.

'If you hadn't led her on she would never have got into such a state,' she said. 'Men always do that. How can you expect women not to turn nasty? You were perfectly unscrupulous about it.'

'I was undecided in my own mind,' he said apologetically. 'You yourself did advise me to make the choice I did.'

'Why should you take my advice?' she snapped. 'What use is it likely to be? I am a failure, am I not? Two sons dead, one in some foreign country before he'd proved himself at all, one by his own hand. By his own hand. What could be worse than that?'

'It is a terrible tragedy,' he said. 'But one thing I do know: Sir Aylmer was a good man.'

'Of course he wasn't a good man,' she rasped. 'Good men don't kill themselves. Can't you drive any faster?'

'We shall soon be at the main road,' he said. 'We shall be able to go faster there.'

'I thought I should die quietly,' she said, 'at peace, with the sun shining outside and my duty done. What sort of death can I die now? He allowed himself to be overcome, totally overcome. He didn't have the strength to bear the knowledge, to bear the requirements of love, to bear the imperative upon man to create out of chaos and out of carelessness his God in his own image. If anyone should have known, Aylmer should have known. But he didn't know. And so the others win, the other impulses in his own blood. That was what shook him so, you see, that Philip and Cynthia were his own blood. What a failure. What a failure.'

She sat straight-backed, gazing out of the window, speaking into the tube but never looking at Moberley's broad uniformed back in front of her.

'No one can say I don't face facts,' she said. 'And if I am expected to face facts and not feel the bitterest anger, well, then too much is expected of me. Too much was expected of Aylmer, too, I know that, but Aylmer should have been equal to it. I am too old. But he had everything on his side. Too much was expected of him. Of course. But he should have been up to it. What else is love for? How many times must I ask you to go faster?'

'I shall be able to now,' he said soothingly. He turned the Silver Wraith on to the main road.

She leant forward urgently. 'Now see what we can do. For God's sake let's have some speed.'

He saw her face in the driving-mirror.

'Are you sure you're feeling all right, 'm?' he said.

'Of course I'm all right. Drive faster.'

The car gathered speed. He felt the power of it, but it gave him no pleasure. She was behind him all the time, crying, 'Faster!'

He heard a sort of coughing sound, and said again, 'Are you all right?'

'Of course. Faster,' gasped the voice.

He drove as fast as he could, wanting now to get her home. They touched seventy-five, the main road empty, the lovely car, sedately chauffeur-driven, the old lady in black behind: seventy-five down hill and she still croaked, 'Faster'.

When he had turned off the main road he said, 'Shall I stop a moment?' worried about her. But she said, 'No. Take me home. Don't stop.' And once on the way he heard her say again, 'Faster'.

When they reached home, she had fallen forward off the seat and lay in a heap of black clothes on the floor of the car. As soon as he lifted her out he knew that she was dead.

He carried her upstairs to her room and laid her on her bed. The family were sent for. He told them what had happened. They stood round the bed. Moberley stood at the foot of the bed, his cap crushed in both his hands. In better times she had laughed at him, saying in her harsh voice, 'You overplay the part of the devoted servant. I believe you have all sorts of black thoughts about me secretly.' His cheeks were covered with tears.

Chapter Twenty-four

The rumours about the war and the rumours about Aylmer's death merged in our minds. They say Edward Grey will resign if we don't support France—they say it was all to do with money—Landsdowne and Bonar Law have promised Asquith their support—if he hadn't killed himself there'd have been another Marconi case—the German Embassy has offered a guarantee—it was all something to do with his wife—no, it was the Irish—well, the Buckingham Palace conference has failed, hasn't it? Doesn't that just show?

And then the Sunday newspapers reporting that German troops had crossed the frontiers of France and Luxembourg; and people pouring back to London; and Grey's speech on Monday, and everyone agreeing he had done very well.

They say there will be a run on the banks for gold—there will be bread riots—collapse of credit in November—they say Aylmer Weston foresaw it, couldn't face it—it was his wife, she was a suffragette, she was having an affair with the nephew. And then the first of the Belgian refugees began to arrive.

I never knew who else realized the cause of Aylmer's death. Old Mrs. Weston had told Edmund, and Edmund, much later, told Alice; but for Kitty the thing was always a mystery, an inexplicable collapse. It took her a long time to absorb it, and then there was the war. She was very pretty at that time. Charleswood was turned into a convalescent home and Kitty became a nurse. There are photographs of her taken at the time, her demure smooth face framed in her neat nurse's cap, as good as gold. None of the little flirtations she had with the patients ended satisfactorily. The men went back and were killed, or stopped writing, or had not told her they were married. She turned, being passionate, a little sour, and, being sensible, a little tough; so that when, after the war, she did go into politics, she was not as effective as she might have been. She was an aggressive Labour Member, rather noisy and bossy, making tremendous issues out of small wrongs and failing somehow to match up to the requirements of large ones. She got fat too; she liked food. She did not marry. Men found her too uncompromising, and she ordered them about too much. She lived in a pretty cottage not far from Charleswood, and devoted herself to her various causes and to the rearing of a particularly ferocious breed of Norfolk terriers. She had a lot of friends, who used to come and stay with her: she was a loyal and witty friend.

I do not think that Violet knew about her mother and Philip either. Other people did of course, in the way that people always do somehow, but it is easy to remain ignorant of something as totally unexpected as the truth would have been to Violet or Kitty. Violet and Wilfred were on their honeymoon in Deauville when they heard the news of Aylmer's death, in a telegram from Edmund. They came home at once; and then of course Wilfred was recalled to his regiment. He was killed at Le Cateau in November 1914. Violet nursed at the convalescent home all through the war, and afterwards married again, quite happily I believe, and had several children.

Edmund volunteered for the Army as soon as possible, and the women were left to organize the convalescent home. Cynthia was not much use at first, because she had relied so much upon Aylmer and felt lost without him. That was partly why she pursued Philip so desperately; she thought he might take Aylmer's place. But she had resilience, and when she found she had lost Philip, she pulled herself together and ran the convalescent home with efficiency and charm—and guile: her patients were the most pampered in England. She was adept at obtaining for them on the highest level special privileges, special food, special services. In some funny way, too, she got special patients: the best-looking, the gayest, the sons of friends, the heroes. And since she was getting older and had lost her husband and her lover, she took anything that was offered by way of consolation. She was not notorious, or in any way embarrassing, but I suppose she did, for what that was worth, lose her reputation; and after the war she did not see so much of the friends she and Aylmer had shared, but moved in different circles and more or less supported a whole crowd of people rather younger than herself; and then when she died, some time in the thirties I think it was, there was something about drugs—not that I believe for one moment that she had taken her own life, but there was an implication that she might have been relying rather on stimulants, and the papers made much of it, printing photographs from the days of her fame and making out that she had had a terrible fall.

I believe she did see Philip again, during the war, in London, but I don't think anything came of their meeting. It was soon after that that he married Ida.

Philip did not re-join the army because it appeared that there was something wrong with his eyes, but he had something to do with some government department during the war, which turned out to be useful afterwards. As a matter of fact I believe he was one of the earliest 'war profiteers', and certainly after the war he did make his fortune, and became a big financier, and meddled in behind-the-scenes politics, and got his peerage. At the end of his career he was rather too closely involved with the pro-Hitler faction and might have found things awkward, if he had survived, but, perhaps fortunately, he died in 1938 at a comparatively early age. Ida divorced him after a year or two of marriage, and he had several other marriages, none of them very successful; but he had everything he wanted in every other way, and perhaps that was what he wanted too, variety. His last wife was quite pretty and much younger than he was.

The war was rather a relief at first. It seemed appropriate after our own private disaster.

Of course we thought, as most people did, that it would be over in a few months. Edmund particularly was desperate to get to the fighting before it was over. He welcomed the war more than anyone, because he was so distressed by what Philip and Cynthia had done, and by his father's death, and he thought that a righteous battle could somehow cleanse the air. He thought that Honour had come again, and all that. It seems silly now, but a lot of people thought it at the time.

Edmund got on to Philip's Army friend, little Smallpiece, who managed to get him commissioned in his own regiment in a matter of months. Little Smallpiece himself was sent to France at the end of 1914 and was killed in his first engagement somewhere on the Franco-Belgian border. His commanding officer was killed before him and he led the men back into the attack as he had been taught, his little feet pounding the shaking earth with rightful pride, and was killed and got his posthumous D.S.O. Edmund had a longer war.

Alice went with Cynthia and Violet and Kitty to see him off at Victoria Station the first time he went. There was a band playing and the horses were excited and had to be backed on to the train, and the General came along in plumes and all the men cheered and all the women cried. It was very grand and brave and though we cried we would not have wanted him to stay behind. That was in the early days, before repetition had robbed the farewells of their glamour and before the daily casualty lists had become part of our lives.

Edmund and Alice corresponded all through the war, and he spent his leaves at Charleswood, where she was nursing. He had some idea that he ought not to marry her until the war was over, but it was generally accepted, though never exactly stated, that they were engaged. His letters changed over the four years, from the early ones, rejoicing in the idea of the battle, to the ones which hardly mentioned the war but spoke only of afterwards and Charleswood, and then to the ones in which he wrote at last, 'Something must have gone wrong,' and 'We out here may not be much use when it is over,' and 'There's been a mistake.' There were probably hundreds of packets of letters like that in different parts of Europe after the war. The story of all that, and of his last leave with Alice, and of her feeling that this time they had not been able properly to communicate, this story does not belong here. It doesn't belong anywhere really. Anyway he was killed in 1917 in the Battle of the Somme and there may have been a moment between the time when the piece of shell hit him and the time when his intestines and stomach were draped across the branches of a dead tree and his dissociated head and legs sank in the mud to be trampled on by his advancing troops, when the thinking part of him could think, Thank God.

Alice finished the war at Charleswood, and then went back to look after her old parents in Ireland. She started a small school there, which brought her much satisfaction, though it was a financial failure.

Chapter Twenty-five

And I, I suppose, was Alice; but it was à long time ago.

Sometimes I think I was closer than that, was Kitty, abandoned by her father, or was one of those girls, a bridesmaid, part of the picture, running in the garden, hiding behind the trees, shading myself under a foolish hat from the sun which shone on a world which was mine. Because I, Alice, was always an outsider; an admirer, but from the outside; it was not my world. It was theirs, and particularly Aylmer's, their representative. And I remember old Mrs. Weston's talk of love, and its requirements and our ignorance, and her dying bitterness against Aylmer.

But I am old, and out of touch, so how can I make generalizations? Besides, I had hardly begun to take in what I was seeing before the war broke out, and my lessons were left unlearnt. I sit in my distant Irish house and read the papers and think, What are we coming to? like any other old woman, and think, reading of a boy lying bleeding between East and West and the world watching and no one moving. If Aylmer Weston had not killed himself this would never have happened. So much did he seem to me to stand for, so much does his suicide seem daily to recur.

Because, as I said at the beginning, this is a private fable, and if it is also about something that happens or might happen all the time or anywhere, and if it is also Ida's fable about Adam and Eve or man's idea of life, and Mrs. Weston's about the impossible demands of love or man's idea of man, that is nothing much to do with me. People make little myths out of the deep discoveries of their lives, one way or another; it is an instinct. And those few months were the vital ones in my life. I do not wish to apportion blame or praise, or seem foolishly to regret the passing of an age which was full of faults; only, for me, had Aylmer not killed himself, had the war not come, we were going to build a kingdom of love. And if you say Aylmer's death was nothing to do with the coming of war, the answer is that the failures are parallel, and that anyway this is a fable, as I said.

* * *

I am Alice on a grassy bank in the autumn sun of 1914, holding in my hand my first letter from Edmund, and with a soft stone trying to write on the back of the letter the name I am thinking of, which is love. I have written L O V and there is Kitty, walking up towards me from the house, and I must tell her that little Smallpiece has been killed and she will be sorry because he amused her and was kind.

'Oh Kitty, I am afraid I have something to tell you.'

She sits at my feet, admiring the future.

'I know. It is that we are all about to be destroyed.'